Las Mujeres Hablan

An Anthology of Nuevo Mexicana Writers

Edited by:

Tey Diana Rebolledo
Erlinda Gonzales-Berry
Teresa Márquez

ISBN 0-929820-00-2 (paper back)

Published by *El Norte Publications*.
    P.O. Box 7266, Albuquerque, New Mexico 87194.

The publication of this book was made possible by a grant from the New Mexico Arts Division and by private donations.

El Norte Publications is the publishing arm of *Academia*, a non-profit corporation whose goal is to preserve and share the culture and art of New Mexico.

Cover painting *"Rojo"* by Tina Fuentes.

Typography by *El Taller Media* (labor donated).
    P.O. Box 4102, Albuquerque, New Mexico, 87196.

Para Nuestras Abuelitas, Madres, Hermanas, Hijas.

Romance de la niña del sombrero negro
Black and White Photograph—Maya Gonzales Berry

Table of Contents

v

Nuestras Familias

Nuestros Vecinos

Nuestros Paisajes

Las Mujeres Hablan

Contributors   206

INTRODUCTION

"Mujer que sabe latín no tendrá ni marido ni buen fin," (the woman who knows Latin will never have a husband nor come to a good end). This dicho, prevalent in Spanish, represents symbolically some of the cultural constraints which affect Hispanic women who write. Knowing Latin, in medieval times, was a symbol of the formally educated person, one who could read and write in cultured civilized language, not the vernacular. It was believed that education of this sort would be an obstacle to the perceived real role of women: devotion to husband and family and to good works. In the hard ranching, farming, and trading society that was New Mexico from the seventeenth century well until the twentieth, women concentrated on survival. Preference for formal education was given to male children who were sent to school in Mexico and, later, to the Eastern United States. While girls were sometimes educated at home and a few from the privileged classes were sent to schools such as Loretto Academy in Santa Fe, the dicho quoted above still wielded some influence as they were to specialize in the gentle arts: music, embroidery and domestic duties. Many women in New Mexico were unable to read or write or even to sign their names on legal documents.

Nevertheless, lack of formal education does not denote lack of creativity, or of the systematic organization, in a creative way, of the world that surrounds one. The oral tradition of songs, religious and secular, cuentos, dichos, recipes, commemorations and recitations of great events pervades every Hispanic household in New Mexico from the earliest days to the present. Within this tradition, women had the reputation of being accomplished storytellers. They were familiar with the great lore of various cultures in the Southwest and passed it on to their children and grandchildren. What Hispanic family is not familiar with the dichos presented by Ciria Montoya in

ix

this anthology? In parallel fashion recipes are part of the woman to woman tradition. Passed on from mother to daughter, it was not the recipe in itself which solely represented the passing on of culture in terms of food and its preparation, but also important was the historical and ritual significance of the cultural context in which the food was prepared and served. This total context then would pass into the oral tradition. It is significant that in the 1930s and 1940s when New Mexican Hispanic women began to write down autobiographies and cultural history in response to a social environment they perceived as diminishing their cultural traditions, one of the strategies they employed was to collect recipes and to narrate, in addition, the cultural context of the food preparation. This can be clearly seen in Fabiola Cabeza de Baca's *The Good Life*.

We suggest that the written literature of Hispanic women in New Mexico is an emerging literature: one which begins to document a long oral tradition. As one Chicana writer has said, "We are beginning to write down, for the first time, our mother's stories." As such this literature has certain features that continue to denote communal "orality" and which give it a special voice. The dichos and recipes are one aspect of this orality. The cuentos of things that happened in village and small town life are another. These cuentos are marked by special characteristics such as attention to detail, careful descriptions of people and places, local idiom, and, often, by a sense of humor. Tales of the supernatural abound (along with the requisite witches, curanderas, and brujas) but are often treated with ironic humor. Such is the case in Josephine M. Córdova's "Bruja Story" and Elva C. De Baca's "Witches." The esteemed position of older persons in the family and in the community is shown by the great respect they are accorded in these tales for their wisdom and knowledge gained through experience. The viejitos and viejitas figure predominantly in cuentos and in biographical stories. Their lives, their words, their example live on in the cultural tradition. When these cuentos pass from word of mouth into the written literature they are often transformed by the creative process. "Vecino Vicente" by Marian Baca Ackerman is a good example of the transformation of the communal tradition into the written one.

In an emerging literature, biography and a sense of capturing the past in order to understand the present become essential to interpreting culture. In the 1930s to the 1950s Nina Otero Warren, *Old Spain in Our Southwest*, Fabiola Cabeza De Baca, *We Fed Them Cactus*, and Cleofas Jaramillo, *Romance of a Little Village Girl* wrote autobiographical tales which attempted to legitimize Hispanic culture by emphasizing that which was Spanish. Today we also recognize our Indian and Mestizo roots. We need to understand that these early writers were just beginning to express resistence to domination imposed by an encroaching Anglo culture. The emerging self, the portrait of "myself" as a young woman, is an important part of this biographical/autobiographical trend. It can be seen in the early literature mentioned above as part of a nostalgia for a cultural past the writers deemed threatened. A great deal is glossed over, and there prevails the notion that the past was better than the present. Contemporary writers are more reflective of the elements that have made them the adult persons they are. Erlinda Gonzales-Berry in "Rosebud" shows how society attempts to restrict young girls so that they will become acceptable female adults. One suspects, however, that this has not been a completely successful strategy. Much of the poetry in this anthology is also reflective and autobiographical and examines the elements of growing up. María Dolores Gonzales, for example, reflects on the influence her names, particularly the Dolores, has on the child, María Dolores. Rosalie Otero in "The Closet" depicts the struggle of a young girl to find a space of her own, and the ingenious way in which she accomplishes it. The continuing element of orality is again present in these growing up stories and poems.

Also represented in this book is the influence religious images have had on these women and the struggle to free themselves from such images or to transform them into new images. Demetria Martínez' work fits in the tradition of a long line of Chicana artists and writers who have questioned, accepted, and recreated the image of the Virgin Mary into one that women can live with. This dialogue with religious symbolism has been an important facet of a battle to free ourselves from restrictive imagery. The change in attitude does not deny tradition, but it does insist that the images be supportive and positive rather than negative ones.

As Yvonne Yarborough-Bejarano has stated, "Chicana writers must overcome external, material obstacles to writing, such as limited access to literacy and the means of literary production, and finding time and leisure to write, given the battle for economic survival." This is certainly true for the writers in this anthology, most of whom write in their "spare" time. But perhaps a greater obstacle in their quest for an authentic voice has been the fact that despite their biculturalism, their lives are often dominated by the mainstream media. Nonetheless, what does sustain them and gives this anthology a special identity is Hispanic culture, tradition and family, plus the struggle to maintain that cultural identity in a changing world. These themes are dominant throughout. Yet within these themes we also discover new approaches, new perspectives. Predominant among them is the female voice: it shouts, it laughs, it transgresses taboos. It describes what it doesn't like about the world, it rebels, it is ironic. Above all it is exploring and writing: not just tradition but, of course, that too. Writings on women's sexuality, perspectives on birth and abortion, the abuse of women, difficult family relations open up multiple aspects of women's lives. Interesting in this particular collection are the stories and poems on fathers for, as has been observed elsewhere, contemporary Chicana writers have tended to focus on mothers and grandmothers.

Two other special features in this anthology are worthy of observation. Many of the poems and stories are written by various members of the same family. Sometimes the relationship is cross-generational, as in the case of Ciria (mother) and Gina (daughter) Montoya; the Chávez sisters (Denise and Margo) and their mother Delfina; mother-in-law, daughter-in-law (Josephine M. Córdova and Kathryn M. Córdova); sometimes it represents the same generation as in the case of sisters Erlinda, Gloria and María Dolores Gonzales. Wonderful as it is to know that various members of the same family are writing, the reader is also allowed to compare perspectives and attitudes within a single family. Moreover, we call attention to the fact that although many of the writers included in this text are published authors, for others this anthology represents their first publication. It seemed to us particularly important to cultivate these emerging voices.

There is a strong interrelationship between literary and visual images. Chicana artists have a long tradition in New Mexico. They have been weavers, santeras, potters, painters and photographers. We are delighted to be able to include in this anthology a small selection of the various artists living and working in New Mexico. Their visual images compliment the written word and reinforce the images found in the textual selections. Like the writers they may focus on the traditional or experiment with mood, imagery and perspective. The question of female identity ranges from the closeness of the three comadres photographed by Linda Montoya to the defiant self portrait of María Dolores Gonzales to the ironic romantic by Maya Gonzales Berry. Bernadette Rodriguez' portrait of her mother as a child reflects a loving memory of family; Tina Fuentes' forceful expressionistic female figure on the cover suggests sexuality and the powerful emotion of woman. Margaret Herrera Chávez' delicate wood block of the first communion contrasts with Delilah Merriman's symbolic landscape. Soledad Marjon encapsules the irony of female identity with flower symbolism entertwined with sexuality and the written word, and Ana María Mastrogiovanni depicts the female body as embedded in landscape.

Finally we must call attention to the use of language. We have chosen to publish the texts in this anthology in the language in which they were submitted. Both Spanish and English are used and we hope the readers appreciate the richness of our culture. Through language these writers try to define their place in the symbolic contract. As Julia Kristeva has noted, "If the social contract, far from being that of equal men, is based on an essentially sacrificial relationship of separation and articulation of differences which in this way produces communicable meaning, what is our place in this order of sacrifice and/or of language? No longer wishing to be excluded or no longer content with the function which has always been demanded of us (to maintain, arrange, and perpetuate this sociosymbolic contract as mothers, wives, nurses, doctors, teachers), how can we reveal our place, first as it is bequeathed to us by tradition, and then as we want to transform it?" Certainly this is where the dicho, "Mujer que sabe latín..." is being transformed. As New Mexican Hispanic women articulate, define and transform their reality through stories, poems, and, yes, even recipes, they not only reveal but also transform their place and we are all the richer for it.

Tey Diana Rebolledo

Acknowledgements

A special thanks to Paul Chávez who gave us permission to print the wood block of Margaret Herrera Chávez. We appreciate all the efforts in type-setting by Laura Lewis and Roberto Roibal who donated most of their labor, and to Yvonne Chávez who helped coordinate the correspondence and keep track of both writers and editors. To Cecilio García-Camarillo, President of the Board, *El Norte Publications*, a special appreciation for his suggestions, patience, and good humor.

The Editors

Tradición Oral Y Memorate

Communion
Woodblock Print—Margaret Herrera (Chávez)

Josephine M. Córdova

Bruja Story

En una aldea al norte de Nuevo Méjico tuve el placer de ser maestra por cuatro años. Me decían mis amigas, no vayas a enseñar escuela en esa aldea porque hay muchas brujas y se aparecen los muertos. Muy contenta acepté la tarea porque yo quería pruebas de que existían brujas.

Pues sí, mucha gente me platicaba que alguno de su casa estaba embrujado. En la casa donde me bordaba, me señalaban las casas donde yo no debía de visitar. Después de conocer a mis alumnos empezaron a venir los padres de familia a hablar conmigo. Todos parecían tan buenos, tan amables, que no podía yo creer por un momento que hubiera brujas en esa comunidad.

El señor donde yo me bordaba me decía, "en esa casa que usted visita le van a embrujar. No esté yendo usted a comer allá," pero pensé porque no puedo ir cuando esas gentes son amorozas y buenas, y qué tortillas hacía la señora de casa. Pensé, vale más ir y comer agusto y más que, me embrujen.

Cultivé una amistad tan fina en ese lugar que nunca he olvidado el cariño que esa gente me mostró.

Recuerdos

Me decían mis amigas
No te creas de ese amor
Porque si tú lo recoges
Vas a vivir con dolor.

Ni los ríos ni las sierras
Nos pudieron separar,
El siempre fue cariñoso
Nunca lo pude olvidar.

Pasaron ya muchos años
Y ya Dios nos separó
Pero quedó muy contenta
La familia que dejó.

Mi familia es hermosa
con alta educación.
Son morales, son benditos
Dios les dio su bendición.

Un sacerdote bendito
Me lo mandó el Señor,
Siempre guía mi camino
Y me trata con amor.

Gracias le doy a mi Dios,
Porque me dio larga vida
Para guiar a mi familia
Que está de Dios bendecida.

Traba Lenguas

De Guadalajara vengo
jaras traigo y jaras vendo.
A real vendo cada jara
A que cara jara vendo.

Dicen que yo he dicho un dicho
Tal dicho no he dicho yo
Y si lo hubiera dicho,
Muy bien dicho fuera el dicho
Por haberlo dicho yo.

Vamos a ver dijo un ciego
Lo que un mudo le decía
Y un sordo salió a escuchar
Pa' platicar otro día.

Explicación: El ciego no podía ver
　　　　　　El mudo no podía hablar.
　　　　　　El sordo no podía ver.

La Bruja Alta Gracia

Había una señora en una aldea norteña que se llamaba Alta Gracia. Era una señora chapa y gorda. No tenía la pobre mujer en su semblante nada atractivo. Nadie la trataba con cariño. Tenía que haber alguna razón porque la gente no la quería. Por mal nombre le llamaban la hechicera.

Esta pobre mujer tenía muy pocos alimentos. Dependía en los vecinos para que le dieran de comer. Durante el día caminaba por las veredas recogiendo hierbas. Llenaba su saco de hierbas venenosas. La gente le decía la diferente, pero nadie hacía mofa de ella porque le tenían miedo. Era una hechicera.

Al caer el sol entraba en su hogar, revolvía lodo o soquete con paja muy fina. Comenzaba a hacer monos o muñecos parecidos a la gente que no le daba de comer. Como bruja que era, usaba alfileres y las clavaba en los monos. Al siguiente día se oía en el pueblo que alguna persona estaba embrujada. Muchas personas sufrían mucho porque esta mujer las había embrujado.

Ella tenía un yerno que la cuidaba y sabía lo que estaba haciendo. Una noche salió ella a andar por los caminos y cuando volvió, llegó a la puerta vuelta un perro. El yerno sacó una pistola y mató al perro. El siguiente día entraron al aposento de la bruja. Estaba muerta con una bala en la cabeza.

Así terminó el cuento de la hechicera.

The Heavy Cross

My mother was born on May 4th, 1867, during the turbulent days when the Indians were raiding the Spanish villages.

Although Kit Carson had dedicated his life to bringing peace between the Indians and the Spanish, a few years before the Indians were still hostile and there were many tribes who still fought to get their land back.

Among the most hostile tribes were the Navajos and the Mescalero tribes.

When my mother, María de las Nieves Martínez was four months old, her parents, Julian and Josefa, lived in Mora, New Mexico. There Indian raids occurred frequently. In August, 1867, there was a raid on my grandfather's ranch.

My grandparents' oldest child, Manuel de Atocha, was playing in the patio with a playmate, Bernadino. The youngsters were enjoying themselves when a group of Indians on horseback grabbed them and kidnapped them.

One elderly lady, a neighbor, ran to Grandma's house to let her know what had happened. The neighbors ran to the field to call my grandfather, but all efforts to find the little ones were in vain.

My poor grandmother almost lost her mind with grief over her lost son.

María de las Nieves, who now was four months old, was handed over to a doctor and his wife. Dr. and Mrs. Gandert kept María de las Nieves more than a year to help bring her up.

After all these unfortunate and sad events happened, my grandmother, who had been a very kind and energetic women, changed to a very cold, desperate person. She grieved over her lost son and no one could console her.

She had in the past been a very loving wife and mother, but now she blamed her husband because he had not searched enough. My grandfather, Papá Martín, as he was called, suffered in silence.

Since my grandmother's parents lived in Arroyo Seco, Taos County, Juan Julián and Josefa decided to move back to where they had lived before.

They possessed a large farm and a very fine home. They had four more children, but no longer did Josefa utter a kind or loving word to my poor grandfather. He occupied himself tending to his farm, and he, as a farmer, made a good living for her and also for his children.

My grandfather was a very kind and considerate man. He loved his wife and family very much, but what happiness can a man find when he has a nagging and inconsiderate wife?

The adjustment and beautiful relationship that they had worked for was all gone. There was nothing left but despair and sorrow.

My grandmother's parents, Joaquín and Encarnación, had brought up their family with great love for Jesus and the blessed Mother Mary. They were fervent Catholics.

My grandmother pleaded with the Baby Jesus to bring back her Manuel. Wasn't Jesus also called Immanuel? What crime in life had she committed that Jesus refused to hear her request?

In her despair, this poor and desperate mother decided to steal the Baby Jesus. She warned the Blessed Mother that if she did not bring her son back home, she would never return the statue of the Baby Jesus to its niche in the Arroyo Seco Church.

She took the statue and hid it in one of the crevices in El Salto del Agua in

the mountains of Arroyo Seco. There behind a huge rock, she knelt and
prayed, and in her sorrow, she cried:

> ¡Virgencita de los campos
> Traéme a mi hijo Manuel.
> Yo te entregaré al tuyo
> Cuando lo traigas a él!
>
> Santo Imanuel de Atocha
> Si me traes a tu tocayo
> Te llevaré muchas flores
> Durante el mes de Mayo.
>
> Si tú, madre, no me ayudas
> Creo que tengo razón
> También tu hijito estará
> Cautivo en esa prisión.
>
> Si tú me traes a mi hijo
> Algún día te he de dar
> A uno de mi familia
> Que te sirva en tu altar.
>
> Mi gente te ha servido
> Con humilde devoción
> Un muy gran favor te pido
> No desprecies mi oración.

She and her little dog Golilla came back after hiding the beautiful statue.
The dog was her only consolation. Golilla seemed to understand why she
suffered so much, for hadn't Golilla belonged to her little son before he
was stolen?

In a way, her family was neglected. If it had not been for her parents and
her devoted husband, she probably would have lost all her children. Out of
seven, four survived. She had two Leonores. Both died during the strife.

For many, many years, she lived in Arroyo Seco. This lonely couple till-
ed the fields and raised many animals. Their home was always well provided with food and clothing. Their shelter was one of the very best. Whenever
an animal was butchered, she shared the meat with all her neighbors. Their

four children were brought up in a very moral atmosphere. They learned and prayed the rosary every night during their lifetime.

After their children got married and left home, this poor couple was left all alone. My grandfather went blind, and my mother and father took him in. My grandmother went to live with Josefita, who was her oldest daughter.

They spent their lives praying. They drifted apart and neither one cared where the other one went.

My grandfather passed away at the age of 85 in 1912, and my grandmother lived to be 95 years old. She passed away in 1927.

For several years, the little girl whom she had neglected when this historical incident happened, took care of her until she died.

At the time of her death, she was blind and had lost her mind. She was bedridden for five years.

It is interesting to know that my grandmother gave her precious belongings, blankets and jewelry, to the gypsies who came by occasionally, in hopes of finding the whereabouts of her lost son.

My grandparents lived a very sad life. This was the enormous cross that they had to carry with them until the time of their death.

Elba C. DeBaca

The Lady In Blue

This story is about a beautiful nun who instructed the Indian people of the southwest in the Catholic faith.

María de Jesus de Agreda was born in Spain on April 2, 1602. She became a Franciscan nun and is the author of "The Mystical City of God," a biography of Our Lady. This was dictated by our Blessed Mother herself.

She had wonderful visions. One day she was shown a vision of the Indian people of the Southwest. She was shown how they had lived in darkness since the time of Noah. It was revealed to her that soon these Indians would be converted to Christianity. She begged Our Lord to make her an instrument in their conversion, and her prayers were heard.

For eleven years—from the year 1620 to the year 1631, she bilocated to the southwest.

She made over 500 visits and visited many different tribes of Indians. She instructed them in the faith and told them that soon missionaries would come to take care of their spiritual needs.

Although she spoke only in Spanish, the different tribes were able to understand her. She performed many miracles in their presence. The Indian people referred to her as "The Lady in Blue."

When the Franciscan missionaries arrived in New Mexico, they were very much surprised to learn that many of the Indian people had already been instructed. On questioning them, they discovered that "The Lady in Blue" had already taught them about Christ and had made them promise to seek out the missionaries when they would arrive.

In the year 1629, Fray Alonzo de Benavides, who was superior general of New Mexico, was conversing with some missionaries who had just arrived from the old world. He heard a noise and looked up. About 50 Indian men were coming to the mission. They had told him that they came from "Titlas" or Texas and that "The Lady in Blue" had sent them to seek missionaries.

Father Alonzo had shown them a picture of a Franciscan nun who had worked among the Indians. He asked them if this was "The Lady in Blue." They replied "The clothing is the same but the face is different. 'The Lady in Blue' is much younger and very, very beautiful!"

Well, then Father Alonzo greeted the Indians, he told them that he had good news for them. He had missionaries to send them. He sent Fray Diego and Fray Juan de Salas with them.

As they neared the place where the Jumano Indians lived, they were met by a procession of Indians. The leaders were carrying large crosses.

The missionaries questioned them and discovered that they did not need instructions.

The missionaries then asked how many of them wanted to be baptized. They all raised their hands. The mothers raised their infant's hands.

The Archbishop elect of Mexico, Don Francisco Manzo y Zuñiga, was wondering what to do. He had received two reports, one from Spain and one from New Mexico.

The one from Spain was from María's spiritual director Fray Sebastian. María had revealed everything to him and in his report, he asked the Archbishop elect to investigate the conversion of the Indians by a white woman.

The second report from the missionaries in New Mexico informed the Bishop that the Indians had been converted by a nun known only as "The Lady in Blue."

After thinking it over, he sent for Fray Alonzo and asked him to find "The Lady in Blue" in the New World.

For eight long years he searched in vain. Finally he made a journey to Spain. He visited Father Bernardine. The Superior knew about María and he directed Fray Alonzo to her. She told him about her flights and described everything accurately.

He was amazed to discover her in his native Spain instead of in the New World!

Witches

I'm going to write about four different witches who lived in different villages and at different periods of time.

The first witch was a fledgling. She had just been initiated into the witchcraft rituals. She was told to say the magic words, "Sin Dios y sin Santa María," (Leave God and his Mother out) when she practiced her lessons in flying. One day she was practicing in the privacy of her home, when she forgot the magic words. She became more and more confused and she said, "De viga en viga!" (from beam to beam). She kept bumping her head on the beams and finally fell to the floor!

The second witch was also a novice. She was practicing her flying lessons in her back yard. She too panicked and instead of saying, "Sin Dios y sin Santa María," she said "Ave María Purisima!" She fell at that instant and broke her arm. She told everyone that she had fallen from a ladder, but everyone knew better!

The third witch had the habit of turning herself into a coyote and roaming the countryside.

One day two fellows on horseback spotted the coyote and gave chase. The coyote ran so fast, that its tongue was hanging out. For a couple of minutes it was lost from view. When they finally caught up with it, there under a tree, sat the witch panting and with her tongue hanging out!

The fourth witch would turn herself into an owl. One night a man from that village was awakened by an owl. He decided to shoot the owl and put an end to the noise. He shot it on the leg and next day the witch was sick in bed with a bullet wound in her leg!

The Devil

In a certain village lived a man who was very wicked. His wife was a saintly woman.

The man was in the habit of calling on the devil and asking him for different things.

One day he was in desperate need of money. He called on the devil and the devil appeared. The man said, "I need some money badly. Will you give me some?"

The devil asked, "What will you give me in return?"

The man answered, "I will give you my soul."

The devil laughed. It was a weird, horrible laugh—horrible enough to chill the bones. "Your soul!" He said, "why I already own it! I want your wife's soul."

The man agreed. That evening he came home in an unusually good humor. He told his wife, "Get ready. We're going on a journey. I will come for you in a couple of hours."

Well, the woman was curious, she wondered what he was up to. She got ready and when he came back, they started on their journey. On the way, the wife saw a church and she begged him to let her go in and make a visit. He thought to himself, "what have I got to lose. I'll let her go in for a few minutes."

The wife knelt in front of the statue of the Blessed Mother and she started praying. The statue came to life and the Blessed Mother told her, "You stay here until I return, but please lend me your shawl."

The Blessed Mother joined the man and he was in such a hurry, that he failed to notice who his companion was, also it was very dark that night.

When they were nearing the place where the devil was, they heard a horrible shriek "not her, not her! That's not your wife!" With those words he disappeared leaving a strong smell of sulphur!

The man repented and led a model life after that.

Ciria S. Montoya

Dichos de José María Sánchez (my father)

1. Somos como los fríjoles, unos para arriba y otros para abajo.
   (We are like beans, some are on top and some are on the bottom).

2. Unos nacen con estrellas y otros nacen estrellados.
   (Some are born a star while others are born seeing stars).

3. Házte el tonto y come con las dos manos.
   (Pretend you are a fool and eat with both hands).

4. Los dichos de los viejitos son evangelios chiquitos.
   (The saying of the old ones are like little gospels).

5. Quien no tiene suegra ni cuñada está bien casada.
   (They that have no mother-in-law nor sister-in-law are married well)

6. Dios da almendras al que no tiene muelas.
   (God gives almonds to those without teeth).

7. No es desgracia ser pobre, pero es muy inconveniente).
   (It is not a disgrace to be poor but it is very inconvenient.

8. Primero es comer que ser Cristiano.
   (Eating comes before being Christian).

9. Amor de lejos para pendejos.
   (Love from afar is for fools).

10. El que sale a bailar, pierde su lugar.
    (He who gets up to dance, loses his place/seat).

The following recipes were used by Ana María Sánchez and her daughter Ciria S. Montoya for serving at weddings, fiestas, baptisms, Christmas and for any special dinners served. (These recipes were also used at the wedding of Regina Montoya (my daughter).

Arroz Con Leche
(Estilo Nuevo Mexico)

2 Tazas de Arroz	1 Taza de Azucar
4 Tazas de Agua	2 Tazas de Leche (Evaporada)
1 Cucharita de Sal	4 Huevos
2 Onzas de Pasas	1 Cucharita de Vanilla
2 Cucharitas de Canela Molida	

Hervir el arroz en agua y sal por 15 minutos. Añadir pasas, azucar y leche. Separar los huevos y añadir las yemas y vanilla al arroz tibio. Bata lo blanco de los huevos y ponga arriba del arroz y rociar con canela.

Rice Pudding
(New Mexico Style)

2 Cups Rice	1 Cup Sugar
4 Cups Water	2 Cups Milk (Evaporated)
1 Tspn. Salt	4 Eggs
2 Oz. Raisins	1 Tspn. Vanilla
2 Tspn. Ground Cinnamon	

Boil rice in water to which salt has been added for 15 minutes. Add raisins, sugar and milk. Separate the eggs and add yokes and vanilla to cooled rice. Beat the egg whites and spoon over rice and sprinkle with cinnamon.

Chiles Rellenos
(Estilo—Nuevo Mexico)

2 Libras de Rez	3 Huevos
1 Libra Chile Verde (Seco)*	1/2 Taza Nuez de Piñon
1 Taza Ceboya Cortadita	1 Cucharita Clavo
1 Cucharita de Sal	1 Cucharita Nuez Moscada
1/2 Taza de Pasas	1 Cucharita Orégano

Hierva la carne. Mientras que la carne está cociéndose, remoje el chile verde en agua fría hasta que esté blandito. Quítele el rabo, las semillas y membrana. Fría la cebolla, añadir sal, pasas y nuezes. Después que la carne se enfríe, muela con el chile y las pasas. Añadir specias (empalma). Revuelva bien. Forme en bolas el tamaño de un huevo chico. Ruede en harina.

Separe las yemas y los blancos de los huevos y bata los blancos y añada las yemas y bata hasta que esté espeso. Ponga las bolas de carne en el huevo batido y fría en aceite caliente hasta que estén dorados. Desecar en toalla de papel.

*Nota: Chile elado se puede usar en lugar de chile seco.

Chiles Rellenos
(New Mexico Style)

2 Lbs. Beef	3 Eggs
1 Lb. Dried Green Chile*	1/2 Cup Piñon Nuts
1 Cup Diced Onions	1 Tspn. Cloves
1 Tspn. Salt	1 Tspn. Nutmeg
1/4 Cup Raisins	1 Tspn. Oregano
Cooking Oil	

Boil beef. While meat is cooking soak green chile in cold water until tender. Remove seeds, stems and membranes. Sauté onion, salt, raisins and nuts. After meat is cool, grind with chile and raisin, add spices and mix well. Shape into balls the size of small egg (oval shaped). Roll in flour.

Beat egg whites until stiff; then add egg yokes gently and beat until well mixed. Dip meat balls into egg mixture and fry in hot oil until golden brown. Drain on paper towels.

*Note: Frozen green chile can be substituted for dried chile.

Irene Barraza Sánchez

Memorias de Tomé

On my last winter visit to the old farm house in Tomé, I drove carefully as the first snowfall of the season was beginning and the road was becoming a blanket of whiteness.

I arrived safely (con las gracias de Dios). Nana, of course, greeted me "mi hija—que bien que estés aquí" and added her usual hugs and kisses. We sat and had a chat over hot café con leche in the small, but cozy kitchen. The old farmhouse, made con adobes y terrón, was always comfortably warm.

As I watched Nana add more wood to the cookstove, I could feel the warmth of the stove as well as the glowing warmth that Nana always held for me. Being the old woman's only granddaughter, we shared a special love and appreciation for one another. the sweet smell of canela warmed the heart, and the stomach soon began to stir with anticipation too.

The natural smells of a New Mexican feast became very evident. I knew instinctively that Nana must be making capirotada for dessert.

Soon mi abuelito arrived with snow flakes blending into his grey and thinning hair. Mi abuelito Ramón always seemed serious, but his leathery face grew soft and lit up when he saw me. He gave me the familiar hug and pat on the back—"¿Cómo estás mi hijita? Bien." "Bien, Papá Ramón, ¿y usted?" "Aquí no más."

Papá Ramón and I chatted while Nana began to mix flour into dough for her delicious tortillas. I watched as she placed the blackened griddle on the wood stove. She let the dough rest a few minutes and then began rhythmically rolling perfectly round circles from each mound of dough. Nana had learned the art of tortilla-making when she was a very young girl. As each tortilla cooked and blistered on the griddle, the smell was enticing.

In a rocking motion, Papá Ramón then began his familiar estoria which he

17

loved to tell over and over since it fascinated all who listened. It was about a gold mine supposedly owned by 'John the Soldier' located somewhere in the Manzano Mountains near the Comanche Canyon area. He remembers so vividly that day as he was herding his flock of sheep through that familiar area. It's almost as if Papá Ramón is transported back in time to that very day as he tells the story, his leathery face so intent. He says he remembers stumbling across mining activity—he remembers the pick and shovel so clearly. He purposely marked the spot with a cross made of old cedar posts and wire.

When Papá Ramón returned home that evening, with so much excitement he relayed to his family the incident. The next day with his youngest son, Jesús, Papá Ramón approached the very spot where the pick and shovel were located and they found no gold mining activity, no pick or shovel; they were unable to locate even his cross made the previous day. Since there is no logical explanation, the legend de la "Mina de Juan Soldado" remains a mystery.

Nana then interrupted and said "la comida está lista." We all went into the cocina and of course there was the traditional New Mexican feast of green chile, papitas con frijoles y tortillas and for dessert, capirotada.

Such fond memories will always be cherished—especially through some of Nana's generation-to generation handed-down recipes, such as:

Capirotada
(Bread Pudding)

1 1/2 cups sugar	12 slices stale bread
1 tablespoon cinnamon	1 cup raisins
1 cup chopped nuts	Whipping cream (optional)

1. In large skillet over low heat melt sugar down to syrup, stir constantly.
2. Tear bread into pieces; place in large casserole dish; sprinkle with cinnamon. Add raisins and nuts.
3. When sugar has turned to syrup, remove from heat. Add 1 cup water and place on low heat until all hardened sugar becomes liquid. Pour over bread.
4. Bake at 350 degrees about 25 minutes.
5. Serve warm with whipping cream. Makes 4-6 servings.

Carol Usner

Tesoros Escondidos

"Oye, grandma" le dije yo, feliz de verla otra vez alegre, "no tienes unos cuentos para mí?

"Qué cuentos, hijita. Ya te he dicho varios. Sabes que no me acuerdo de ellos. Tu mommy ya los tiene escritos todos, toditos, en aquel libro que ella escribió, ¿sabes?"

Sentada en su cuartito, comenzamos a platicar. En los últimos dos años ella ha sido menos fuerte por causa de una caída que sufrió. Se recuperó, pero todavía no ha vuelto a alcanzar las fuerzas que tenía. Su visión se pone menos aguda, pero su espíritu está todavía alegre, fuerte, sensible. En el invierno mi abuelita vivía con nosotros dejando su casa en Chimayó cerrada hasta la primavera cuando ella volvía, muy contenta de poder estar en su casa. "No hay como la casa de uno;" dice ella. "No se siente bien en las casas de los otros. No sé por que. Es que aquí en Chimayó está mi vida, mis amigas...¿Sabes? No hay como la casa de uno".

Mi abuelita vivió en Durango, Colorado, y San Francisco, California, pero la mayor parte de su vida ha vivido en Chimayó. Cuando era niña vivió con su padre y sus hermanas. Después de casarse vivió con su marido cerca de la casa de su papá, en una casa que él (su marido) y ella misma construyeron. "Did you know I built this house? Your grampa and I. These cabinets are mine. Do you like them?". Su inglés es bonito. Ella ha sido bilingüe desde su niñez. El papá de ella era tejedor y les enseñó a sus hijas el arte. Mi abuela entonces tejía bastante. Le enseñó a su marido a tejer también. Ella fue la primera de su familia en salir para ir a la escuela en Santa Fé. Ella aprendió bien el inglés y tenía muchas amistades entre las otras muchachas y sus profesores. "Todo el mundo me quería. ¡Como me querían! I'm not bragging, mi hija, la verdad es que me querían a mí."

Nacida en 1898, ella ha visto mucho, desde los "Carros de Bestias (horse and buggies) de su papá, hasta los "Mercedes Benz" que tiene su hijo menor. Ha vivido desde cuando había caballos, animales del rancho, noches largas, inviernos largos, con cuentos de su papá, otoños llenos de las cosechas de chile, manzanas, frijoles, hasta hoy con los carros, los supermercados, noches con la televisión, la radio para cantar, pero todavía hay chile. Tiene que haber chile.

"Oh grandma, ¡este chile caribe está bueno!"

"Te gusta? Me alegro. Todo mundo me dice a mí que le gusta el chile caribe."

"De todo lo que haces, grandma."

"Oh sí. Las tortillas, el pan, las sopaipillas, tu grandma sabe cocinar."

"Sí, sí, abuelita."

Mi madre siempre ha aprovechado de los cuentos de mi abuela. Mi abuela tiene una voz como una canción, una larga canción, que lleva a uno hacia sueños, hacia tierras alejadas con princesas, reinas, reyes, brujas, frailes, mundo de fantasía, pero no tan lejos. Mi madre y yo la escuchamos bien, pues la amamos. Nos arrulla su música.

La Niñez Rescatada

La Brown Eyes
Graphite Drawing—B.K. Rodríguez

22

Margo Chávez

Manina

Manina knew only one tune on the piano. If she had ever known any others, she had forgotten them, or she didn't like them as much as this one. It was a jumpy Mexican number. Although she hit a lot of wrong notes, especially as she grew older, her enthusiasm brought her without hesitation to the crashing end.

If I try to describe her now, my portrait can only come out blurred, filmed over by the inevitability of passing years. She was small, maybe only as tall as I was then. She had a hump on her back, but she was not bent over double as was the hunchback woman in the Paris metro corridor who had a view of only her feet and their tired marching and of thousands of feet unattached to bodies or lives. That woman in the metro corridor, if she wanted to see what was before her, had to twirl her head around on her neck like a discarded doll and strain her eyes to adjust to this unnatural and unaccustomed perspective of the world. Manina was only slightly bent over. I can almost fix the features of her face, but only for myself. If I try to attach to them words, they disperse like a reflection in water, held for only seconds before a rude movement comes along to dispel such an illusive image. There is nothing else I can tell you about how she looked except that her skin was nut-brown, her hair white, and she wore longish dresses.

She had been playing the piano at our house the day she fell. Someone would often ask her to play. Manina was flattered and was always ready to pound out her piece. I wonder now if she had written it herself. Perhaps the asker really did want to hear her play that day. I may have been in the kitchen when we heard her cry. But I, in remembering, have become the omniscient narrator and I stand behind her shoulder in the living room as she gets up from the piano, walks around the edge of it to pass through the dining room

23

into the kitchen. She trips on the edge of the small piece of rug covering the floor furnace. Perhaps she slipped on the border of the furnace, her foot expecting to feel the carpet, finding instead the smooth metal surface. We ran in to find her next to the furnace in a small heap, moaning a high-pitched and still strong "ay,ay."

Manina was always around in those times of my childhood when we went to visit Mama Toña. Mama Toña lived in the house that her children had built for her, but Manina, childless, lived behind it in a strange wooden house. I went in her house a few times. Around it there was no yard, or what could be called a yard. Under the Texas sun it takes work to cultivate any more than dirt and pebbles, rusted metal and tumbleweeds. Inside Manina's house I remember a piano as dilapidated as the house, and a brown clutter from which I can separate no one object. Mama Toña and she were sisters; Manina must have been older. Mama Toña was my grandmother. I don't think I ever knew much more about Manina, about the things that children wonder about: why she had a hump on her back, why she had no children, why she chose to stay in that house darkened by age.

What I know is hardly enough to construct a tangible personality, unless substance can emerge from memory. And the memory of a little girl is formed from shadows in dark wooden houses. Yet she has substance for me still. Her name was Cleofas Telles, I don't know why we called her Manina. She liked wine, especially when it was sweet. One summer that we spent at Mama Toña's, the doctor prescribed wine to increase my flagging appetite. I wouldn't drink it, but it slowly disappeared from the refrigerator. Manina went to church every day early in the morning. It wasn't far, only across the two railroad tracks that passed in front of the house, and then a few more blocks. My mother told me that Manina had an obsession with time. In her life, it seemed that one minute was like another, but she always needed to know what time it was, as though naming the passing hours gave them some significance. Perhaps she was on her way into the kitchen to glance at the clock above the refrigerator that day she fell. She was cheated because she was never able to fix that moment in time.

From then on Manina lived with us. She didn't go back to her dark house in Texas, but stayed with us in New Mexico, living in a high hospital bed like a crib in the room that had been my father's study before he left us. She wore white hospital gowns, the kind that never cover you completely and leave you embarrassed until pain takes away your shame. Various women came to take care of her. They were from Texas or Ojinaga, just across the Texas-Mexico border. Belsora was the best; she stayed the longest and sometimes brought her funny-looking little boy with her. He watched television, and Belsora and my mother changed Manina's rubber sheets, moved her into a new position despite her wails, and later fed her like a child.

If Manina at first was waiting for the hours to pass until she could get up and walk to the piano again or to the clock above the refrigerator, she eventually became impatient and a slow despair crawled into her mind. She would call me or my sister. Neither of us wanted to go in there because by then we knew what she would ask. She would tell us to take the rail off the bed and put a pillow on the floor so she could roll onto it. She only wanted to leave her hospital bed and we couldn't let her.

No one ever told Mama Toña what had happened to Manina. After several strokes, part of Mama Toña's brain was shut off. It had damaged her speech; the little notes she sometimes wrote had the same pattern of incoherence, but within them, you could glimpse an idea you understood. Finally Mama Toña came from Texas to visit us and she was led into Manina's room. The two sisters spent a lot of time holding each other's hands after that. At some point I know Mama Toña cried, with wordless sorrow that understands and doesn't. Mama Toña may have come several times to visit; I don't remember how long it was before no one led her anymore into the room that had been Manina's. No one ever told her that Manina had died. I don't think she ever asked, but she must have known why she was not taken into that room again.

Manina's life had become one of waiting to die. We knew it at least, but no one could tell what Manina still understood. Her hope, her intelligence had slipped away with the hours that used to be so important to her. If she was impatient now for anything, we couldn't tell. Mother and Belsora would go in, change her sheets once more, shift her from one unhealed sore to another, and my mother would come out, silent, her face crumpled by sadness.

We knew Manina was dying soon, so we were there, on that bright day, all of us, and the doctor who knew he was there only to watch, and the priest who had come once before. I held the container with the priest's oil. I watched

Manina's face as he rubbed the oil on her eyes, her nose, her mouth. Death, a passage into limitless time, may have meant nothing to me then, for I was so young. Even later, when I saw several more faces that were unnatural in their death, felt many hands whose feel had lost anything human, and kissed many cold foreheads, it was solemn, but incomprehensible and far-removed from me. I always felt sorriest for the ones left behind, as I felt sorry for my mother that day.

Then I looked at Manina's face. I saw the tears that squeezed out of her eyes which had for a long time been closed. Why was she crying? She had not known anything for weeks. I wondered what she knew now that made her cry. If she was dying and she was sorry, I was sorry for her too. But if it was something else she knew, I wondered how she knew it. In my missal there was a prayer for a peaceful death. Sometimes my mother would hand me in church a holy card with the prayer written on the back. I always thought of Manina. Since then I have wondered what voices she heard in her seemingly peaceful death. Or was it only the voice of her sorrow, or relief, or anger? Which did her tears represent?

After we took out the hospital bed, that became my room and we later sold the piano.

Erlinda Gonzales-Berry

Rosebud

(excerpts)

I

You might say we were a wild bunch, especially for being girls. Though we spent part of our childhood on a ranch, dad tried to keep us indoors, away from the corrals and animals. Wasn't fit for ladies to be out in men's territory, he said. Our job was to learn to keep a good house, like our mother, and to make good tortillas. What pop never knew is that when he and the hired hand had to make a trip out to pasture or into town, my sisters, Victoria, María, Luisita, and I headed straight for the corral, climbed the barn roof and took turns jumping to the ground. The possibility of broken limbs was not out of the question. Not one of us however, would ever admit to being a gallina, so jump we did.

High on the list of favorite pastimes was killing snakes. Red-racers were especially fun because we had to run all over chasing them, and it wasn't easy to make a good hit on the run. They often got away. Bull snakes were easier but no fun at all—they just laid there and let us blast stones at them until their tiny heads caved in. I remember an unusually long and fat one that kept squirming and wouldn't die. I finally got a great big rock, stood right over it, and delivered the death blow. I really felt kind of rotten about the whole thing but just shrugged my shoulders and said "heck, racers are more fun." We then headed for the pasture to look for horned toads.

II

True, we lived on a ranch, but we didn't have a lot of animals or money. In fact, it wasn't even our ranch. Pop had lost our ranch a long time ago. Actually, he sold it to his brother and we moved to town. We hated town because we had to go to nuns' school. They were all mean, crotchety crones except for Sister Frances John. She was young and kind and she told us great stories about Saint Christopher who crossed the baby Jesus on his shoulders over the raging river and about the host that bled when dropped on the floor. Sister Anthony Marie, the seventh and eighth grade teacher was the worst. She pretty much ran the whole school and always threatened everyone with a good ear-boxing. I had never seen one, so I wasn't quite sure what that was all about. I found out, though, one Holy Thursday.

Monday and Tuesday of Holy Week we practiced for the Holy Thursday procession. I was to lead the third, fourth and fifth graders. That meant I got to wear a flower wreathe and carry a lit candle. I could hardly wait. Everyone would know I was the smartest girl in class. Actually they already knew it because ever since I started school, I won the spelling bee. Truth is, we all won. Consuelo (the nuns tried to change her name to Consuela because *o* is masculine in Spanish they said, but mom and dad let them know in no uncertain terms that they did not approve and would send *Consuelo* to public school if they insisted) wiped out her class, and Victoria and María outspelled the younger wimps. The whole town admired the Martínez sisters, but I think they were a little jealous too because no one else ever stood a chance in the spelling bee.

Anyway on Tuesday Sister Frances John said that right after the "Gloria," we should recite the "Pange Lingua." On Wednesday I was sick and didn't get to practice. What I didn't know is that the group was told that *if* the choir sang we should *not* recite. No one bothered to tell me about the change in game plans, so come Holy Thursday, right after the "Gloria," I lead the little lambs of God in recitation of the "Pange Lingua" while Mrs. Oliva pounded the organ and the choir belted out a Latin hymn. The louder they sang, the louder we prayed. I was determined that we would prevail. After all, wasn't I a Spelling Bee Champ? When Mass was over, Sister Anthony Marie walked right over to me and BOXED MY EARS! Boy, was I embarrassed, and was I ever mad. At recess while Juanita, Suzy and I were getting ready to play jacks, I said some real mean things about Sister Anthony Marie. I even called her a few bad words (if you must know they were: old cow, pinche vieja, and cerote seco) even though I knew I would have to go to confession after school if I wanted to receive Holy Communion on Good Friday. Juanita and Suzy threatened to tell on me, but I gave each one a Cracker Jacks prize and they forgot about the bad words.

When we left town because mom got a job teaching in Rosebud, we were happy to leave the ear-boxing nuns, and all the Catholic parents were happy because their kids would have a chance to win the Spelling Bee.

III

Rosebud was no rose bud. It was more like a rose thorn. There was a concrete school house with three rooms, a mail box, an old abandoned building that was once a store, a house, and a corral with a barn. Actually it was a pretty neat corral. It looked like those I had seen in story books. The corrals we knew from our old ranch had piñon posts lined unevenly side by side. This corral was made from lumber planks and was painted red. We could sit on the top plank like Dale Evans did in the movies and watch the cows. One was a milk cow. I always wanted to milk her but pop wouldn't hear of it. "That's men's work," he would say and that was that. Although we talked about it a lot, we didn't dare approach her udders because Molly was not one of those dumb looking cows with soft bovine eyes. Quite the contrary, Molly had a mean streak in her and liked to bolt at anything in sight, aiming with her horns. I found that out the day I tried to bullfight her.

Summers were a bore in Rosebud. Only pleasant thing that happened was that Connie came home. During the winter she lived with Grandma in town and went to high school. Summers she spent in Rosebud helping dad take care of the wild bunch while mom went away to college. Since mom didn't have a degree, she had to take classes every summer in order to get her contract renewed.

So summers we read a lot and listened to Connie tell neat stories about high school. I could hardly wait to go there myself. I used to day dream about being the smartest and most popular girl in the freshman class and at night, before going to sleep, I imagined myself kissing the basketball team captain. I would shiver just thinking how a kiss might feel. It was quite clear that I would have to wait til high school to find out because the oldest boy in Rosebud Grammar School was in the third grade. I was in the seventh. Kelly

Marie and I were the oldest kids in school. That was good and also bad. The good part was that we could boss everyone else around. The bad part was that we had a lot of responsibilities. One day, for example, one of the first graders soiled his pants and *we* had to tend to him because the teacher (mom) was busy in the reading circle with the fourth grade Blue Birds. Sometimes Kelly and I got to lead the second grade Yellow Birds in their reading lesson because the teacher (mom) was busy teaching Social Studies to the fifth graders. That's how things went at the Rosebud school. Everyone pitched in and helped each other learn. There were grades all right—first to seventh— but they weren't really all that important. What was important was fifteen cheerful kids who every morning sang "O Columbus the Gem of the Ocean" and "A Spanish Cavalier" and who tried, the rest of the day, to learn something about the marvellous world that lay beyond the wind-blown plains of Rosebud.

IV

Once a month on the last Friday of the month the older kids went with Mrs. Green to Amistad to 4-H Club. The idea of spending the afternoon with boys our age drove us gaga. We primped and giggled all the way on the bumpy gravel road. Deep down I had mixed feelings about Amistad. There were only white kids at that school. That was true about Rosebud too. All the kids that were bused in from their ranches were white. We were the only brown kids. But we were one happy family and color didn't matter. It did at Amistad. At least, I felt it did, and I got that feeling from the way kids stared at me and Vicky.

I found out just how much it mattered the day we baked biscuits. Mine turned out light and flaky like they were supposed to. Our group leader was kind and said my biscuits were county fair prize-winners. That made me feel good. I wasn't even thinking about my brown skin when Tommy Bevins came up to me and said.

"Give me a biscuit."

"Gee, Tommy, I'd like to, but I only have one left and I want to take it home to my mom."

He looked at me real mean before he said it: "Dirty Mexican."

I ran to the bathroom and looked in the mirror. He lied. I wasn't dirty. Why did he say it? Why?

When we got home, I gave mom her biscuit and I told her about Tommy Bevins.

"Ay m'ija," she said "forget it. Just turn the other cheek." Mom always said, "Turn the other cheek." "That Tommy doesn't know anything. You're the cleanest and sweetest little Mexican I know." She held me in her arms and kissed away the tears.

V

Of course, mom didn't know about the red racers and the bull snakes. She didn't know about the rock fights either, at least not until Connie told her about the day María came running in with blood gushing from her face.

It was summer and we were specially bored. We decided to build a fort with crates and boxes we found in the garage. After it was built, we decided to tear it down and to build two small forts so we could have a war. María and I were the Huns and Vicky and Luisita were the Goths. The stone shower began. When we ran out of ammunition we would wave a white hankie and take time-out to gather stones. When we were ready to resume the war, the side that took time-out blew a whistle and pelted the enemy fort with rocks.

Forts and war were forbidden the day María caught a rock in the nose. That was the same day our embroidery lessons began.

Elida A. Lechuga

Remembrances

"You must hold very still," the anesthesiologist said as he tapped her back searching for the opening near the proper vertabrae. I'm a tree, she thought, a very tall, very old tree, a tree that no longer moves in the wind but stands tall and stately, unaffected by the elements. The idea worked. María did not move as the needle pierced her skin and the catheter was forced into her spine. "You must hold very still" became a litany in her mind, her brain supplying the unsaid words: or you could be paralyzed, or it could kill you.

"Done," the doctor proclaimed. Did he sound relieved too, María wondered. "You will feel a slight sting as I put the medicine into the catheter," he explained.

María wanted to laugh but did not dare. A slight sting would be welcome after the pain that she had just been through. This must be a very special baby she wanted to say to Anthony whom she couldn't see but whose presence she felt. He should have been holding her, she thought, not the nurse.

The slightest sting straightened her back into a full sitting position. The nurse must have seen the fear in her face. "It's okay to sit up now," she said still holding María's hands tightly. María caught a glimpse of her husband and wondered if she looked as afraid as he did. Oh Tony, she thought, should you even be in here?

"We want you to lie down before the medicine takes effect," María heard the doctor say and soon the nurses were shifting her body back to the head of the bed, but María no longer felt a part of that. Something strange was happening to her. Something, maybe the catheter, maybe the drugs, had awoken memories that María had thought were long dead.

She was no longer thirty-year-old María having a baby but seven-year-old Marielena and she was lying on the old outdoor swing, her head in her grandmother's lap. Smelling of dirt, summer days, and witch hazel, her grandmother's rough hands gently rubbed the bump on her forehead where the baby horse had kicked her.

Grandmother constantly warned Marielena and her brother of the dangers of crossing the barbed wire fence to the field where the neighbors kept their horses. They will step on you, she would say, they will run over you and then kick you. But Marielena was fascinated by the horses, their coats shiny and beautiful, their legs strong and powerful as they chased each other in a game of horse tag. Marielena stood near the fence and watched them. People on television touched horses. Mr. Ed even talked to people. All she wanted to do was pet a horse.

That summer she had her chance. A baby horse joined the others in the corral. He was brown as ditch water after a summer cloudburst and he had a white rectangle covering his face from his eyes down to his nose. He was so much smaller than the other horses, not very much bigger than Marielena herself. Surely she could touch him. She watched him for weeks until one day when her brother was at their cousin's house and her grandmother was roasting green chile in the kitchen she slipped between the line of wire. One of the barbs caught at her favorite blue and white checkered dress and it almost made her go back. She stepped back into her grandmother's yard but she was still stuck so she stepped over the rusty wire once again and yanked herself free leaving a piece of material the color of the Albuquerque sky on the fence. Stepping into the field, she realized how much the fence had protected her, the horses could do anything they wanted to her, but they didn't even look at her.

Quickly, she found the baby horse. It was just a few steps away, its back to her. I'll just go up and touch it, she thought, and then I'll go back to Grandma's. Walking toward it with her hand outstretched, Marielena saw its ears twitch and its tail move just a little bit. It seemed to get bigger the closer she got to it.

Her hand was a few inches from its backside and that was the last thing she remembered until she woke up and saw the blue sky above her and felt a pile of horse poop under her back. Slowly she sat up and touched her head. It hurt. She could feel a big bump forming in the middle of her forehead. The horses were at the far end of the corral. Standing up slowly she walked to the fence and climbed through, careful not to snag her dress again.

Her grandmother stood in the shade of her house watching her. "Te dije," she scolded her pointer finger wagging sternly at Marielena. "I told you," she repeated in English, shaking her head slowly.

"Her blood pressure's dropping too fast," María heard a woman say. "Go get the doctor," the voice ordered. Opening her eyes, María saw the student nurse who had been observing her labor step quickly out of the room.

"She said she couldn't breathe," the nurse reported as the anesthesiologist rushed into the room.

Who said she couldn't breathe, María wondered. They're talking about me. I don't remember saying that. Leave me alone she wanted to say, but the nurse was putting a mask over her face. "Breathe deeply," the nurse said as she adjusted the elastic strap behind María's head. María wondered if they put vaseline on their upper lips to keep smiling.

She watched the anesthesiologist inject something into her I.V. He patted her shoulder. "You'll be just fine," he assured her. "I'll see you in surgery."

So, the caesarean was a certainty. What kind of operation will I use to get this kid out of the house twenty years from now, María wondered.

It was summer again and Marielena, her brother, Andy and her two cousins, Eddie and Frankie, were walking down the dirt lane following their grandmother away from her house. She never said where she was going and they never asked. They just followed.

Eddie ran into the field that bordered the dirt road and Frankie followed. The alfalfa ready for its second cutting was almost as tall as Eddie and covered Frankie completely. "Bet you can't find us," they taunted Andy, the youngest of the group, as they fell down and were hidden by the tall, purple-flowered stalks of green. Marielena wanted to run after them but she was the oldest, almost ready for second grade when they weren't even in kindergarten, so she stayed beside her grandmother.

"Quítense de la alfalfa," their grandmother's husky voice boomed across the field. The laughter stopped and the boys quickly retraced their steps over plants they had unwittingly trampled when they first ran into the field. Selling the alfalfa supplemented their grandmother's Social Security income and she guarded the fields surrounding her home as closely as if they were graveyards. The more broken plants there were, the fewer bales there would be, and that meant less money for candy orange slices and grandchildren's Christmas presents. Nobody knew this better than Marielena who had been punished the year before because she had stomped out a large circle of alfalfa to have a tea party with her dolls and a few ladybugs. Now she bent her head down and smiled secretly to herself, waiting for her grandmother to yell at the boys again, waiting for her to send them back to the house. That didn't happen. Marielena wanted to protest, say how unfair it was that they didn't get in trouble, but she knew it would do no good. "They are boys," her grandmother would say and probably send her back to the house. She pressed her lips together and stared at the ground so nobody could see how angry she was. It was then she noticed that her grandmother wearing her Aunt Carmela's new blue canvas tennis shoes. Sundays were the only day Marielena had ever seen her grandmother wear her own shoes.

"Where are we going," Marielena dared to ask.

"La cequia," her grandmother replied tersely and continued to walk slowly and steadily, the pace of a woman who has seen most of her life pass and conserved her energy for the years to come.

"But why didn't we go to that ditch," Marielena asked pointing behind them.

"We're going to the big ditch," grandmother replied.

The boys had heard and they were whispering to each other. The ditch. The forbidden ditch. And now their grandmother was taking them to the ditch.

Marielena's mother had often talked about playing in the ditch when she and her brothers were young children. Nobody had swimming lessons, they just jumped in. The youngest had to stand lookout and yell a warning if any turds might float by. Marielena asked why she couldn't play in the ditch and her mother had said because she didn't know how to swim, making logic out of illogic as only mothers can.

The big ditch, when they reached it, looked deep and flowed ominously fast. Assuming their destination had been reached Marielena and the boys looked at the ditch for a few seconds and then turned, ready to go back. Their grandmother was walking farther down the wide ditch bank. "Ay está el Rio Grande," she said, indicating with a sweep of her arm the vast expanse of cottonwood trees across the ditch.

The children all looked across in wonder. Who would have thought that their grandmother lived so close to the river. And still their grandmother walked farther until she came to a place where there was a grove of young willows. Without a word she took the knife she had somehow hidden in her ever present apron and began hacking at the tallest and straightest saplings.

"Here," she said, handing the first severed tree to Marielena.

"I want one," Eddie shouted and the two others took up the cry. Soon the ditchbank was witness to a chorus of greed. The boys fought over who would get the next stick. Eventually everyone had at least two sticks in hand and Marielena realized why they had not been left behind when their grandmother went to the ditch. She needed them to help carry the long sticks. If she had told the boys she had a job for them, they would have balked, hiding behind the pump house so they could play with Frankie's matchstick collection instead.

"What do you need the sticks for?" someone asked.

"For the lana," their grandmother replied and everyone laughed. Sometimes they had to clean the lana from their bellybuttons.

'For the lana,' became the battle cry as the little boys and one little girl brandished the sticks, some much taller than themselves, all the way home.

María opened her eyes to the acrid smell of ammonia. "You should be awake for the birth of your child, Mrs. Hernández," a voice said. "I've never seen the epidural affect anybody as strong as it did you." The masked owner of the voice came into María's line of vision. A nurse. She looked like a blue monkey, the pressed out paper mask protruding into a mouthless snout.

"Where's Tony?" María asked as it suddenly dawned on her that she was no longer in the birthing room.

"Here I am," he replied. He was sitting with his head very close to hers. "Where have you been?"

"The big ditch," María replied and Tony laughed. "What's going on here?"

"You're going to have a baby, Tony said absentmindedly as he stood up and looked over the curtain that was positioned over María's chest.

"It's a girl," Dr. Nelson proclaimed.

"I'll let her swim in the ditch if she wants to," María said quietly to herself.

Several months later, after she told Tony about the birth memories as she now called them, he asked, "What did your grandmother use those sticks for?"

"She had these mattresses that were filled with wool, lana, and she wanted to wash the wool. She ripped up all the mattresses and washed the lana in these big tubs outside. After it had finally dried, she used the sticks to beat the wool so it would fluff up again."

"She should have used a dryer." Tony said and smiled.

"I told her she should buy new mattresses."

Tony stood up and walked to the cradle where his daughter was sleeping. He smiled down at the child and commented, "I'm sure glad you didn't want to call her Lana."

Reynalda Ortiz y Pino de Dinkel

Las Monjas

Todas visten de negro
Visten de negro, hábitos y velos negros
Velos aforrados de blanco pero negros
Todas con rosarios a la cintura
Rosarios largos de cuentas negras como los hábitos
Cuelgan de las cinturas de las monjas los rosarios
La uniformidad monótona de velos negros con los hábitos
Nada quita que las monjas tengan distinción
Las hay de semblantes rayados tiernamente por los años
Las hay de semblantes rayados y las hay de caras sin líneas
La frescura de las caras que apenas han tocado los años
Se entreteje con la marchitez de las otras caras
Con las que ya han aprendido a amar a Dios y vivir con él
A su lado; todas las monjas viven así, con grandioso afirmar
De amar a Dios y vivir con él a su lado.

The Nuns

All are dressed in black
They wear black, black habits and veils
Veils lined in white but black
All with rosaries at the waist
Long rosaries of black beads, black like the habits
Hang from the waists of the nuns
The monotonous uniformity of black veils with dark habits
Does not detract from the distinction the nuns may have
There are those of lined countenance gently stroked by the years
There are those of lined countenance and those of unlined face
The freshness of the faces that scarcely the years have touched
Mingles with the withering of the other faces
With those who have already learned what it is to love God
And live with Him at their side
All the nuns live like this
Live with a magnificent affirmation of loving God
And living with Him at their side.

Rosalie Otero

The Closet

Everyday I am suddenly aware of something taught me long ago—of some certainty and self-awareness that grew out of conflict in my youth. When I was a child there had been many places available for me—for play, for daydreams, for imagination. I could talk to myself, spread out my toys, and escape to wonderful imaginary places. But, as the years went along, the family grew and encroached into my space until there was only my room and the garden. One day, when I was thirteen, my room went too.

It began when my little brother, Mikey, came upon me braiding the corn silk in the garden, running like the devil was behind him. I was engrossed in separating the cornsilk into three even sections, the beginning of a prize-winning hairdo on my make-believe model. I let him know I didn't like his interruption, but he paid no attention to me, and just blurted out, "Tía Rufina is coming to live with us."

That Saturday Tía Rufina arrived. She was old. Her skull shone pink and speckled within a mere haze of hair. She wore orange-brown stockings on her contourless legs and a lavender coat with enormous buttons running down the front. As she rummaged through her purse, she complained about her hat, a gray flannel with tiny purple flowers around the band.

"Mariquita should know better. Mira, she bought me this gray hat to match my canas. Pa más canas. I told her to take it back pero ya sabes estas muchachas. So you can match, Tía, mire las florecitas. Que match, ni match." She pulled out cough drops from her purse which she considered a confection both tasty and salubrious and gave two each to Mikey and me.

40

She had been delivered to us by two of her maiden nieces, Manuelita and Susana. She continued to think of them as young and would often refer to them as "las muchachas de tu Tía Mage." They were ten or twelve years younger than she was. They both had blue hair and black dresses with shiny black beads on the bodice. They were, though maiden ladies, of a buxomly maternal appearance that contrasted oddly with their brusque, unpracticed pats and kisses.

As we dutifully kissed and hugged all around, Doña Maclovia Carson burst into the room in brilliant color and bustle. She was a portly woman with large breasts and skinny legs that made her look like a chicken. She had red hair which she dyed and always wore stacked on top of her head in a donut shape. Large glass earrings dangled furiously as she gestured with her head.

"Cómo estás, Rufina? Hace tanto tiempo that you've been here." She embraced my aunt who winced. Mikey giggled and I pinched him.

"I was hanging out the sheets and saw a car. I thought it might be you and I couldn't let you get away again without saying hello." My mother patiently explained that Tía Rufina had come to live with us.

"Oh, how marvelous! We'll be vecinas, comadre." Then in her usual style, sometimes subtle, sometimes brusque, Doña Maclovia began asking a series of questions, the answers of which she would later embellish as she gossiped with the other neighbors.

"Did you sell your house? Qué lástima, such a nice little house. You have arthritis? I have just the cure." Doña Maclovia considered herself a curandera claiming she had learned the art from her mother, Doña Dominga Sandoval. Mi Minga, as everyone knew her, had a good reputation and people from the community and even from far way places came to her for help. She was too old and feeble now and needed constant care herself, but still every now and then she would wrap herself in her black shawl and place her hands on someone's pain. Doña Maclovia went about the neighborhood handing out remedies for everything from cancer to common colds. The people placed little faith in her cures and would say, "Esta no sabe nada. Nunca aprendió, nomás pa mitotear y componerse la cara."

"Rufina, just mix some methanol and cinnamon and rub it in. Then cover up with a warm blanket and the next day you can do the varsoviana." She let out a raucous laugh and the donut on top of her head shook loose a few red strands.

"Maclovia, can you cure Fleabit? He's been limping all day," Mikey broke in with a pleading expression. He had really done it this time. Not only had he interrupted an adult conversation, equated Tía Rufina's ailments with the dog's, but he had broken the social rule. All adults had to be addressed as Don, Doña, Mano, Mana, Aunt, Cousin, Uncle...and a thousand other appelations indicating familial relationship and the lowliness of the addressor. My mother looked hard at him and then at me. I grabbed Mikey's hand and dragged him into the kitchen. Mikey's puzzled look became a mischievous grin when I scoldingly explained what he had done.

"Well, you didn't have to squeeze my hand so hard."

I shushed Mikey and listened to the cacophonous conversation in the other room. It was perfectly audible because Doña Maclovia was obstreperous and the three tías were hard of hearing. Only intermittently did we hear the mellifluent voice of my mother.

"No, that was Pablita, daughter of Pablo and María. Tu sabes, vivían en Cheyenne," Tía Susana was explaining.

"Hermana de la Josephina, tu vecina?"

"No, no. Cousin to Josephina. She only had brothers."

"You remember, the oldest one was killed in the war and they never returned his body."

"Oh, sí, she was the one who married her first cousin and they had that idiot son, ¿cómo se llama?"

"Manuel."

"Sí, Manuel."

Mikey began to get fidgety. He wasn't interested in geneologies and neighborhood gossip.

"I'm hungry."

"Shshsh....I want to hear about the idiot."

"You're the idiot. I'm the hungry one."

I was torn between bopping Mikey and forever being ignorant of the idiot, Manuel. "You always interrupt at the juicy parts. Go get an apple."

"I want a cookie."

"You brat!" I took a swing at him and missed. Mikey grabbed the package of Oreos and escaped to the TV room.

I missed the whole thing about Manuel. When I got back to listening, the women were on a different subject and I had missed the transition.

"Su vida fue muy triste, muy pesada. Siempre la tenían sembrando, escardando." Tía Manuelita was saying.

"Her father used to call us 'Carajas' especially when he felt we were keeping her from her work."

I wondered what that meant. I had learned a great deal of Spanish from being around grandpa before he died, not like Mikey who didn't know anything, but I did not know the meaning of "Carajas." I made a mental note to ask my friend, Mercy. She knew everything.

Late that afternoon the two tías readied themselves to leave and Doña Maclovia escorted them out acting as if she was sincerely going to miss them.

That night I went to bed in Mikey and Danny's room. Actually, Danny had moved into the room with David and so now that room was really mine and Mikey's, but it wasn't mine. I felt strange, out of place. I couldn't sleep and tried to read, but mother said that I would have to turn out the lights because Mikey was sleeping. I wanted to protest, but it wouldn't have changed anything. I would just have to accept the fact that that's how things were and would remain. I cried softly into my pillow.

One evening I went out to the garden, the only place where I could sometimes be alone. The earth was pale clay yellow and the trees and plants were ripe, ordinary green and full of comfortable rustlings. As I knelt near the apple tree and heard the hollyhocks thump against the fence, I felt the breeze lift my hair playfully and watched the trees fill with wind. I felt a sharp loneliness. The kind of loneliness that makes clocks seem slow. I wondered if anyone could understand what I was feeling. There seemed to be no place for just me.

Our house was comfortable and quite large. Mother and father had been very proud that they were able to purchase their own home soon after they were married. It had been a two bedroom, one bath house, but father had built additions seemingly with every new child. He converted the garage into a large den complete with paneled walls and a built-in entertainment center. Later he enlarged the kitchen and added a bedroom and bath. When Mikey was born, he divided the den into two rooms, the smaller portion became

David's bedroom and the larger side remained the TV room. Still later, father built a large laundry room for my mother which he also divided into two rooms. Half became a pantry-closet. Mother always mourned the fact that the large window was on the closet side and she had to rely on electric lights whenever she did the laundry. Soon after Dad finished that project, however, he surprised Mother with a freezer and the closet became the "catch-all" room. Mother no longer canned vegetables and fruits; she froze everything. I think that was about the same time the kitchen was enlarged with a space for the freezer and a small pantry.

Father loved building projects. When there was no more room for add-ons and enlargements, he began with the yard. Every summer he would feign a fight with the lawn, pull out his wheelbarrow and begin mixing cement. Every summer the lawn became smaller and smaller and flagstone spread in all directions. I was relieved that Mother had insisted that the back yard remain green with space for trees and flowers and a large garden. The grass in the backyard grew wild for the most part and much of the area had been left bald by strenuous play with the neighborhood boys. But even in the back, Father had made a large flagstone patio and walks leading to the garden and the small orchard.

I smiled as I recalled the determination and pleasure with which Father always seemed to work. He'd expect the whole family to inspect and approve all of his projects, which we did dutifully because they were always done well. My mother used to say that when Father nailed something, it would remain that way for eternity. I walked back to the house comfortable with my thoughts. As I neared the door, I heard Doña Maclovia's ringing voice. I stole silently into the kitchen where the adults sat talking.

"Mano Mon is dying. I just went to take him some té de oshá. Anda, Maclovia, see what you can do, me mandó mamá. Pero what can I do? He just coughs and coughs."

"Is Tiófila with them?"

"Sí, pero esa uñas largas comes to see him con interés. She already took some of Pablita's, God rest her soul, best china. And poor Ramona ya tiene los ojos rotos de tanto llorar. I keep telling her that her brother hasn't died yet, but you know." She shook her head and her earrings went into a frenzy.

I knew Mano Mon. We called him "chipmunk" because he always had both cheeks filled with tobacco wads which he gummed down to a fine pulp and spit brown and rich on the street. I'd also never seen such a bald head. It glistened and the boys would say he buffed it every morning, first thing.

He died later that winter and we all went to the wake and funeral. Velorios were always festive times for children; there was good food to eat, the adults were busy, and we could run around unsupervised. Sometimes we would steal into the room with the coffin, peak at the dead person, and run outside to tell the others the horrors we had discovered.

"Mano Mon moved. Really!"

"He's gonna come and get you tonight."

"As long as he's not buried, his ghost is still around."

"You lie."

"I don't lie. My Dad told me that Mano Mon's spirit had gone to our house to say goodbye. The salt shaker fell off the table and nobody was moving it."

"Yes, that really happens. Doña Maclovia Carson swears she heard Mano Mon calling her. Right outside her window."

"She wished." This from one of the bigger boys who grinned lasciviously.

"Ya, she probably hasn't ever had anybody call her." Everyone giggled as if they had some great secret among them. I giggled too, but I felt a sadness for her. She dressed in loud colors and bohemian styles and talked friendly to everyone, but nobody loved her. She didn't have any friends, any real friends. I think my mother was the only person who realy felt sorry for her and tried to be her friend.

"Whaddya think about Doña Maclovia and Inocencito?" The whole group went into hysterics. The boys jostled each other and the girls giggled into their hands.

"A match made in heaven." Floyd, one of the older boys, folded his hands as if in prayer. The rest of us just laughed harder. Inocencito, not his real name, although I don't know if anyone remembered his real name anymore, was a short squatty man with coarse black hair that fell unevenly around his head. He often wore a baseball cap sideways and since he rarely shaved, his wrinkled, weathered face looked dirty. He collected old newspapers and sold them along with the current ones. As if conjured up by our laughter, Inocencito approached timidly. He headed toward some of the men standing near the doorway. He removed the baseball hat and stuffed it into his jacket.

"Se murió!"

"Sí, Inocencito, se murió." That was my father's voice.

"Sí, he was killed. With a gun."

"No, he was sick. He just died a natural death."

"Read about it here." He pointed to the newspapers under his arm.

"Quién? Who died?"

"Pués, era el mero mero de Washingtón. El Presidente. The best we ever had."

The men stood straighter and listened more intently. The President had died? We listened too. My father took the newspaper from Inocencito. The edges were yellowed with age. The front page bore pictures and the story of President Kennedy's assassination. Everyone breathed as if in unison.

"Sí, Inocencito, President Kennedy was killed, but that was almost ten years ago. Where did you find this paper?"

"Ten years ago?" He shook his head not comprehending. He threw his head back in quick jerks in an effort to remove the hair from his eyes.

"Ten years ago?" He stepped through the men and into the house.

"I wonder if he thinks Mano Mon is the President?" Mikey asked.

"He just found that old newspaper. That's what I call being behind the times!"

"Hey, it could be worth lots of money."

The economics of the old newspaper were left to another day; the adults were gathering their children and leaving. Neither Mikey nor I slept very well. Our minds were filled with death and ghosts.

"Lucy, Is it true what they said?"

"No, Mikey, they just wanted to scare you. Go to sleep."

"I don't want to die."

"You won't for a very long time. Now go to sleep."

"Is Tía Rufina going to die?"

"Yes, someday. We're all going to die. Someday."

If Tía Rufina died I could have my room back. I shuddered that I could even think such a thought. I prayed hard that she wouldn't die. "Oh, God, Oh, Mary, sweet mother of Jesus, I didn't mean that I wanted her to die.

Please don't let her die." I felt that by my mere thinking of the possibility, it could happen; it would be my fault.

"Lucy, are you praying? Are you scared?"

"Sh, Mikey, go to sleep. Everything will be okay."

Mikey finally fell asleep, but I lay awake a long time trying very hard to hear Tía Rufina's breathing in the next room.

On Saturday morning Mikey ran into our room squeeling, "Lucy, Lucy, it snowed. It snowed. Will you help me build a snowman?"

"Good grief, Mikey, it's only six o-clock. Why aren't you watching cartoons?"

"Please, please. I'll go away if you promise."

"I promise."

How beautiful the white field in its blur of fallen snow, with the delicate black pencil strokes of trees and bushes seen through it. I stood in front of the kitchen window for a long time. The snow silence becomes hypnotic if one stops to listen. I looked out on the patio and saw the charming lacing loop and circle lacing of Fleabit's tracks through the snow. The dog was racing around, waving her tail.

David and Danny appeared in the kitchen at the same time. They looked so much alike—tall, wiry, with thin lips and large brown eyes. It was hard to believe sometimes, that they could be so different. David was seventeen, intelligent, quiet. He hardly ever talked, usually just gestured or grunted. He preferred to read or listen to music, especially jazz. Danny was fifteen. He was energetic and boistrous, more like Mikey. He loved to tease me, but he didn't get rough with me like he did with David or Mikey.

"What's for breakfast, little mama?" he drawled as he sneaked up behind and tickled me. I squealed. Mother, who had already started heating the comal for pancakes, frowned at us.

"Lucinda, get the bacon from the refrigerator. David, go take the cereal box away from Mikey. Danny, get your coat on and help your father sweep the front walk."

Danny groaned, but he was soon outside throwing snowballs at the windows and the dog. Mother shook her head, but I noticed a small grin.

"You kids, I swear. I should have sold you when I had the chance." She smiled at me and I felt happy to be in the kitchen with her. Mother was a flame that warmed and lit everything around her. Yet she was often, I feel sure, close to exhaustion. She swallowed the unacceptable because it made life so much easier. Hers was a life spent all in giving, spent for others, as the beloved queen of a tiny kingdom. She was a magisterial woman, not because of her height, she was only five feet tall, but because of her bearing and her upbringing. Her love for her children was utter and equal, her government of them generous and absolute.

That afternoon Mikey and I bundled up needlessly since the sun was bright and hot and went out in the field to build a snowman. We put one big ball on top of another, and carved them down with kitchen spoons till we had made a figure of a man in voluminous trousers, his arms folded. While Mikey knelt and whittled folds into the pants and shaped the bottom to look like oversized shoes, I stood on a wooden crate and molded his chin and his nose and his hair. It happened that Mikey swept his pants a little back from his hip, and that his arms were folded high on his chest. We didn't do it on purpose— the snow was firmer here and softer there, and in some places we had to pat clean snow to make a stronger shape. When we were finished, he seemed crude and lopsided, but still suggested a corpulent man standing in a cold wind. We hoped the man would stand long enough to freeze, but in fact while we were stamping the snow smooth round him, his head pitched forward and smashed on the ground. This accident cost him a forearm. We made a new snowball for a head, but it crushed his eaten neck, and under the weight of it a shoulder dropped away. We went inside for a snack, and when we came out again, he was a dog-yellowed stump in which neither of us would admit any interest. During the winter there were other snowpeople that took the fat man's place. Some actually turned out symmetrical and jovial and stood for several days.

It was a long winter and there were rare days when I could escape by myself to some corner of the house. At least in the other seasons I could still visit the garden, but during the winter, I would get cold quickly and couldn't retreat into flights of imagination for chattering and thinking about the chill.

One day spring arrived. The garden had been full of surprises as the spring flowers blossomed, one by one. One morning Tía Rufina wanted to go out with me. She wrapped a wool shawl around her shoulders and leaned on my skinny arm.

"Que jardín tan lindo." She admired the lilacs that were out in profusion.

I felt a sadness about Tía Rufina. She was going from us, little by little. She seemed distracted or absent-minded, but I think, that in fact, she was aware of too many things, having no principle for selecting the more from the less important. She was in the final flowering and meaning of her life, but she would not be dragged into it, protesting, resisting, crying out. She was able to do less, enjoy everything in the present like a child.

"Tan lindo. Tan lindo." I felt helpless and sometimes terribly irritated by her repeating the same phrase over and over as she did. And she had death in the back of her consciousness much of the time. She would often say to my father, "Y que me muero y no me muero y allí estoy."

"Y esa ventanita?"

"That's the broom closet."

"It looks right out here. Such a pretty view. Such a pretty view."

The inspiration came slowly, but then, there it was. I jumped up, my heart thumping, my brain conjuring the perfect plan. I rushed to my aunt, danced around her, hugged her, kissed her wrinkled forhead shouting at her, 'Oh, Tía, thank you. Thank you. That's it!"

She looked pleased. Did she know? Did she understand what I'd been feeling, needing, wanting, all these months? I galloped toward the house leaving Tía alone in the garden. Flushed, blustering, I deluged my mother with every logical and illogical reason I could contemplate. I made promises, resolves. I pleaded until she succumbed.

I finally got moved into the broom closet. It was a tedious affair what with all the junk that had been accumulated in there. Not only did I remove the brooms and mops, but hundreds of paper sacks, plastic bags, old newspapers, rotting potatoes, forgotten boxes, and rags, hundreds of rags—old dirty, small and large. The closet had also become the permanent residence of several microscopic creatures. I winced as I cleaned out sticky cobwebs and miniscule furry nests.

But I was determined to have my own space, so I had pulled down my sleeves—I couldn't bear the feel of cobwebs on my skin—and got to work. All day long the family paraded by.

"What are you doing, Luz?"

"Why are you in there? Are you being punished? What did you do?"

"Hey, Lucy, you found my old T-shirt?"

"Hey, Luz, are you gonna give these newspapers to Inocencito?"

"Lucinda, you are making a mess."

"Luz, can I have this neato albino spider for my collection?" and on and on and on.

I tried to ignore everyone. I had too much to do to engage in lengthy conversations or explanations. Besides, they wouldn't understand.

"You can't live in a closet," Mikey stated emphatically on his twentieth trip past the closet door. He crossed his arms over his slight chest and stood pouting.

"I can so," I shouted back. "Go away and leave me alone."

His eyes misted and he ran off to keep from crying. I felt badly that I had yelled at him. He was the funniest and most enjoyable of the whole family. He had shared his room with me eagerly, happily. He was always ready to talk and eager to learn. Everyday since he started school, he would come home with a new word:

"What are piojos?"

"What's a lumbrís?"

"Tomás said Doña Maclovia had almorranas. What's that?"

"What's a pecoso mocoso?"

Each time, mother would cringe or blush, look at Tía Rufina and either explain or dismiss him abruptly. One day he ran into the kitchen slamming the door behind him and asked, "What is chingado?" Mother turned redder than I had ever seen her. The color started at her neck and raced to her forehead as if she were being submerged in cherry Kool Aid. Before Tía could even get a gasp out, Mother grabbed Mikey and dragged him to her bedroom. Mikey wouldn't say what she had done or said, but I know it had to have been very very serious and he was careful what he asked after that.

On his twenty-first trip past the door I apologized and tried to explain that since I was a girl I needed my own room.

"Besides, now you can have your room all to yourself and you can spread out your toys and play without my bothering you."

"You didn't bother me, Lucy. Don't you like me?"

"Of course I like you. Besides, now we can visit each other. I'll invite you to my room and you can invite me to yours." I tickled him and he ran off to "spread out" in his own room.

The broom closet was small, but it was mine. I arranged my bed under the window, my small dresser at the foot and my father helped me put up a pole for hanging clothes. My mother made ruffled curtains that matched my bedspread, one for the window and a large one to act as closet wall. I arranged and rearranged my belongings and looked out the window at the garden every few minutes. Tía Rufina shuffled in to admire my new room. She brought a large bouquet of lilacs.

"Pa tu cuartito." She winked at me.

Merrihelen Ponce

Los Calzones de la Piña

As children our daily diet consisted of simple foods such as avena, hot oatmeal, potatoes, and tortillas. These foods, and the pinto beans we were fond of were the main staples of our Mexican-American diet. Since most of the families in the barrio of Pacoima had numerous children, our parents bought large sacks of comida: to ensure that if nothing else, the family would always have beans and tortillas. My mother too bought food in large a-mounts such as beans or flour that came in hundred-pound sacks. The beans were kept in their brown hopsacking; the flour however was emptied into a huge can (first washed out and dried) then stored in the pantry along with a sack of potatoes and another of sugar.

The flour was sold under two trade names: Harina de la Piña, which had a picture of a huge pineapple in front, and La Espiga de Oro, decorated with a stalk of wheat. Once the sacks were emptied my mother and our adopted grandmother, Doña Luisa, ripped them apart, shook out the last of the flour, washed and bleached the sackcloth. This was later used to make dishtowels, limpiadores, aprons, or clothing, in particular underwear, calzones for the girls of the family.

My mother, as did most women of the neighborhood, worked hard to clothe our large family. While trying to bleach out the pineapple and wheat stalk from the sacks she would sometimes tire of stirring the zinc tub full of hot water and agua fuerte, bleach, and would remove the cloth before the design had bleached out. She then emptied the tub in the back yard (with the help of Doña Luisa) and hung the sackcloth to dry on the long clothesline. When dry, the sacos would be ironed then laid out on the kitchen table built by my father. My mother and Doña Luisa then cut patterns from newspapers or thin brown tissue paper, similar to grocery bags, laid them atop the material and with great care, cut out underwear or aprons.

My mother learned to sew when in Mexico. However she first learned to cut a pattern in the sewing class under the direction of a teacher at Pacoima Elementary School (which I attended). The class was started by the principal, Mrs. Goodsome, who wanted to teach women of the barrio how to cook and sew "the American way". Among those who enrolled was a neighbor, Juana, said to be very low-class. Muy ranchera. When asked whether she was interested in learning to sew Juana was heard to say, "I don't wanna learn how to sew nothing. All I wanna learn is how to make cak-es." Once assured by the teachers that yes, she could learn to make cak-es and pies— even cookies, she enrolled in class but attended only the cooking session.

My mother would have liked to attend both classes but spoke only Spanish, and was embarrassed to admit she could not understand the teacher's instructions given in English. Soon after she and Doña Luisa quit attending. They preferred to sew at home, and knew how to make patterns using old clothes as a model. When a blouse or dress was not longer wearable, they ripped out seams, ironed out creases, then worked from this. I used to like to watch them work; Doña Luisa busy with the two irons kept hot atop the wood stove, my mother's greying head bent over the Singer Sewing Machine with the foot pedal, one she faithfully oiled and kept covered with a clean cloth.

Although it was common practice to use sackcloth for clothing, no one in the barrio cared to admit a dress or shirt was made of sacos. However, the picture of the pineapple, la piña, was especially difficult to bleach out. Oftentimes the material retained a yellowish tattle-tale color, one carefully sewed towards the back seams. It was because of this that I wound up wearing undies with a picture of a pineapple near the bottom, that unbeknown to me was visible every time I bent over.

For some time, the calzones de la piña had sat in the bottom drawer of the chest I shared with my older sister Trina. I hardly noticed they were there until the fateful day when I ran out of clean underwear and was forced to wear 'homemades'. I tried to be a good sport as I hitched them up. I hated the idea of wearing sacos but hated more hurting my mother's feelings. My mother worked hard to clothe all eight of her growing children; I did not want to seem ungrateful. In addition to cooking, canning and baking 'pan', the sweet bread we so loved, she found time to sew aprons, slips and the underpants we girls were expected to wear without complaint. They were made with love, were well made, "bien hechos," and sometimes trimmed with rickrack. To the Mexican people of our town it was important to at all times appear clean. It was often said: "Somos pobres, pero, limpios. We are poor, but clean."

That day I wore los de la piña to Pacoima Elementary School where I was in Second grade—and in Room 2. This day I was somehow allowed to play kickball, a hard running game with the other kids. This was a great treat. When a teacher knew that tuberculosis was prevalent in a family such as ours, we were discouraged from playing what were called 'rough games,' so that we would not exert ourselves. We were made to sit quietly on a bench alongside the chainlink fence to watch the ongoing games. The other kids knew the reason for this, and would point to us as "los tísicos."

On this day I was picked to play kickball by a teacher who saw that I was a chunky, healthy looking girl with red cheeks who could benefit from the exercise. I quickly jumped off the bench then took my place among the circle of players and began to practice kicking the ball.

Once the game began I kicked with all my might. I ran all around the field, getting in everyone's way, excited at being young, healthy, and full of energy, happy to be playing, happy to be part of the gang. I never gave a thought to the stiff bloomers decorated with a pineapple that were visible each time I kicked the ball.

I played gloriously. I played hard. I played to win. I was so intent on kicking the ball as far as the boys that it was some time before I heard the giggles and saw fingers pointed in my direction. I then realized the pineapple was showing—but didn't know what to do. I kept playing. Soon I felt a loosening at the waistline. The elastic on my bloomers had burst! I could feel them beginning to slide. I was in a panic—and yearned to hear the recess bell.

My underpants however did not fall. My chunky hips kept them up. I then began to hook them up before I kicked the ball. Soon the kids began to call to me: "Mary Helen, Mary Helen." When I turned around they would hook up their dress or pants, then double over, convulsed with laughter. This went on for what seemed like hours, with me hooking up los calzones, my face hot and flushed. I was close to tears when recess finally ended.

I walked back to the classroom, my sweaty hands gripping my dress at the waistline. Wihout a word, Mrs. Paddington, our teacher handed me a safety pin. I took it, went into the girl's bathroom and pinned up my underpants. I returned to class full of dread at having to face my classmates, ashamed to have them see how hurt and embarrassed I felt. But they said nothing, merely avoided my glance.

Once at home I took off the calzones and stuffed them in the bottom of the drawer. I vowed to never, ever wear them again. I didn't tell my mother about this incident but after that began to handwash my underwear to ensure I would never again be forced to wear underpants with a picture of a pineapple at the bottom.

Vicki Lynn Saiz

Here Sits A Girl

Here sits a girl
A little child, who is afraid of the dark,
Of demons lurking behind
Every tree, under every bed.

She runs and jumps into her bed
Instead of giving the devil a chance
To grab her ankle.
She's heard tales of Satan
Manifesting himself
Then disintegrating into ashes.

But she knows if she prays
He won't come into her Holly Hobbie room
He won't sit on her canopy bed
So she begins:
    Now I lay me down to sleep
    I pray the Lord my soul to keep
    If I should die before I wake
    I pray the Lord my soul to take.

There. Now she's safe
No fiery creatures are going to get her.
She can sleep
And dream little girl dreams
Of running and laughing
And kissing her daddy.

But still he watches
Envious of her innocence
Just waiting for the night
She forgets to pray.

Lorraine Torres

¡Ojalá Que No!

—Ándale mi'ja, no andes gastando tiempo. Hoy es el primer día de la escuela y tienes que estar lista para las nueve.

—Bueno, mamá, pero dígame por qué tengo que ir a la escuela.

—Ay, hija, ya te lo he explicado muchas veces y ahora no tengo tiempo ¡Apúrate!

—¡Pero, mamá yo no quiero ir a la escuela! ¡Tengo mucho miedo, qué tal que se me salga el español!

—Mi'ja, se tiene que ser. No te apures, tu inglés está muy bueno. No te va a salir el español.

¡Yo no quiero ir a la escuela! ¿Para qué quiero aprender a leer? Y yo no necesito más amigas. Lo que me da más miedo es que voy a hablar en español. Dicen todos que les dan una nalgada cuando hablan en español. ¡Ay, que miedo! Ojalá que no se me salga el español. ¡Ojalá que no!

Pues parece que es verdad. Claro dijo la maestra que no se iba a permitir hablar español. Si me quedo quietita no tengo peligro que me den nalgadas. Ojalá que pase el tiempo bien rápido.

—¿Puedo andar contigo?

—Shhh, the teacher will hear you!

—No me importa, acabo que ya es tiempo de ir a lonchar.

—But we're still on the playground. Someone might hear you and then you'll get a spanking!

—No me importa.

—Do you like school?

—Poquito.

—I hate it!

—¿Bueno, mi'ja, como te fue?

—Well, mamá, sí es verdad que dan spankings cuando hablas español. Yo tenía mucho miedo. Pero, I did bien.

—Qué bueno, come tu lonche.

—Mamá, cuando I walked a la casa una de mis amigas nuevas was talking español. Ella no tenía miedo que la oyeran hablar español, pero I did, yo creí que iban a pensar que yo was talking español. Y yo no quería que me dieran una nalgada. También me duele la cabeza de tanto oír inglés.

—Mi'ja, mi'ja, no te van a dar nalgadas. Por favor no hables tanto y come tu lonche.

—Sí, mamá, mejor de no pensar de la school ahora.

—Ándale, mi'ja, ya es tiempo de volver a la escuela.

—Bye, mamá.

¡Ay, como me dió lástima por el boy cuando le dió la teacher con la ruler en las manos. Pobrecito, él ni sabía la word en inglés. El pobre ni se dió cuenta que he was talking in español. ¿Por qué es que se enojan tanto? Yo voy a aprender English tan bien que never voy a hablar español, solamente cuando yo quiera. Voy a comenzar a practice hablando solamente el inglés.

—Hello, Mamá.

—¡Hola! ¿Cómo te fue en la escuela?

—Fine, Mamá, but I was scared when the teacher le dió—I mean spanked a boy.

—Bah, que lástima, pobre niño.

—Mamá, starting today I'm practicing my English all the time. No quiero—I mean I don't want to get a spanking.

—Bueno mi'ja, es bueno que quieras practicar tu inglés.

-Mi'ja, ya mero son las nueve ¡Apúrate! No quieres llegar tarde.

I hate school! I hate school! I hope my Spanish doesn't come out. Please, Jesus don't let me get a spanking today. I guess I'm lucky I know English so good! Please don't let me speak Spanish, Jesus! Please! I hate school! ¡Ojalá que no hable español! ¡Ojalá que no!

Nuestras Familias

Self Portrait
Black and White Photograph—María Dolores Gonzales

tesamaechávez

To Dad

It was autumn in Aztec.
I was walking up Old Ruins Road
kicking fallen leaves
when I saw you in greased cover-alls
high off the ground on Ray Atchicin's
Caterpillar grader.

You were sitting straight though the ride
was rough and bounced you about the seat as you
waltzed that Cat of Ray's through the "old bridge"
like an Indian tracking wind.

I yelled and waved my smallness
lost in the roar, yet my swelling heart pumped
by your power and prowess in handling that
huge machine carried me to town in record time.

It is this rugged image of you, Dad,
locked in my brain that's used to judge
any man I gaze upon!

Kathryn M. Córdova

The Legacy of Rainbow

I'll call him Rainbow. He represents their varied cultures, the rich blending of their colors, the treasure at the end of all that is said and done. He means something that is hard to attain, available to few chosen ones, but admired and envied by all.

These comforting thoughts ended María's long cry. It was not for herself that she cried. It was for Carlos and Rufina, her recently dead and beloved aunt and uncle.

Rainbow, the old and valuable white buffalo kachina that was her inheritance, would always represent the great, almost fairy tale love that Carlos and Rufina left as a legacy to all who knew them. Just an hour ago, María's father José brought the revered mounted doll to her as a lasting testimony of love from Carlos and Rufina. Now, María not only had a prize to add to her treasured kachina collection, but a sentimental reminder of a life gone by.

As she sat at her large pine snack bar in the kitchen drinking herb tea and staring at Rainbow, she recalled when she first knew the possession would one day be hers.

Rufina sat smiling at her niece. Even though the seventy year old Rufina moved only with the help of a wheelchair, she moved toward María and gently touched the younger woman's hand. While there was an approximately forty year gap between aunt and niece, there had never been any generation gap. She let María feel her genuine approval as the younger woman openly admired the white buffalo kachina which hung in the living room of the warm adobe apartment. The kachina, adorned with brightly colored leather trim and long white fur, assumed a regal pose in his special place of honor in the room. His lifted head looked straight and proud. In his right hand, he held a small bunch of feathers. and his left hand held a bright red rattle. His body was mounted on a board with red velvet cloth, surrounded by an oak frame.

"You like him don't you?"

"Yes. He's beautiful. You know, some people think it's almost pagan for me to admire kachinas the way I do, but it's an art form, Tía. To the Indians, each kachina has a meaning. It's fascinating, almost like poetry. But I don't worship them as gods."

"I know. Your Tío was half Indian, and he loved this kachina just as much when we bought it in Grants in the early fifties as he did when he died. You know, you have a good, healthy respect for kachinas. Your uncle noticed that about you. He was really proud when you gave him a framed kachina that you had embroidered.

"Well, I didn't know he owned one; and it seemed like something he'd enjoy."

Rufina spoke softly. "Not too long before Carlos died, he and I decided we should leave you our White Buffalo. We knew you'd cherish and respect it. This will be yours some day. Only I'm not going to wait until I die. Let me enjoy it a little longer, and one day, I'll tell you it's your turn to have it."

María wept for a short while, remembering the moment of love she shared with her aunt. But her aunt never lived to give her the doll. Why did her aunt and uncle's lives come to an end? Why the suffering? Why the empty feeling? Perhaps Carlos and Rufina's message from the grave was to remember them fondly, with love and respect. Rainbow is a sign that they are still with María in one, though many varied spirit.

The house was quiet now. Everyone had gone to bed. María became concerned about the picture she presented to her family when José first brought Rainbow to her home. I must have looked like a damn fool, she thought, with mascara running down my cheeks as I saw the doll actually here in my house. Then, I went on and on about what it meant to me to actually have something of theirs near me. But I've really got to present a more positive picture of death. Beautiful memories. That's what they need to learn about their dead loved ones.

The slim, handsome dark-skinned boy with dark brown eyes ran through the area surrounding his father's trading post at Acoma. Carlos never missed anything with his dark, bright eyes, sharp ears and alert mind. He enjoyed his active life. The trading post was the center of activity in Acoma. That, in addition to the fact that Carlos' father was the only Jewish man to hold the honor of governor of the Sky City, made life interesting for the Bibo family.

He had a happy boyhood going to school and playing games with his brother and sister. His mother instructed him in the Acoma way just as his father exposed him to Judaism.

While Carlos learned the Indian and Jewish ways, Rufina busied herself rolling tortillas and cooking frijoles for the large family of brothers and sisters whose mother died at a young age.

Life was happy for Rufina and her husband, as there was much laughter, and even more love, to surround the household of a father and his twelve children. Even though there wasn't much extra money, the family always had whatever it needed for survival.

Known chiefly for her huge, wide smile, rounded cheeks and auburn hair, Rufina had a clear, smooth complexion that was the envy of many women in Santa Fe. Her smile showed quite often, as Rufina laughed heartily at the playful antics of her brothers who loved to play pranks. She also shared many a smile with her sisters as they confided secrets and talked "woman talk," referring to all them as "kid."

The Montoyas, Rufina's family, were well known *fiesteros* in the Agua Fría area. A dance or party always found at least one or several Montoyas in attendance. Carlos was no slouch in enjoying himself either so it was natural that they should meet. Their courtship and subsequent marriage carried with it a zestful love of life, one filled with retirement winters in Guaymas, family reunions, and local and cultural events in Santa Fe and Acoma.

Though childless through their long marriage, Carlos and Rufina *did* have their own children, after a fashion. Taking the little ones of the Guaymas orphanage under their wings, the couple set to gathering children's clothing, donating, and encouraging others to do the same. And then, there were José's kids.

Three children, two girls and a boy, aged ten, nine, and eight, with whom the Bibos lovingly shared time. The two years before José's remarriage were filled with some overnight visits. The children spent an occasional evening playing Monopoly in the apartment basement, which would later be used as their bedroom for that evening. Picnics to Camel Rock, walking Rex, the German Shepherd, watching Carlos play tennis and attending the rodeos all became a treat when José would allow the children to visit. Then, there were also times when José, the children, and Rufina and Carlos would all spend time together, eating and talking.

When José remarried and his family grew, so did the love—and the bond. As the children grew, Rufina and Carlos did what any close aunt and uncle would do—let go. Deep inside, they knew that life would once more be enriched—this time with great nieces and nephews. José's five children each went their way, each pursuing what their heart told them to, but all were irresistably drawn to a loving force—Rufina and Carlos, that unique couple whose love conquered all cultural and religious barriers. The ones who never let childlessness, illness, or any of life's tragedies break their spirit.

Cancer. Not even that could end their bond with the living memories.

"I'm the only Indian who will die without a drum." No. Take Arsenio's drum, made by Red Shirt of Taos. Tears. Shared by Rufina and María at the hospital. Shared by the family after Carlos' death and after Rufina's death. The letter written by little Angela, the great niece, to a dead aunt and uncle, with the theme, "Together Again." The lying in state in coffins and velorios in the Spanish way, the Corn Ceremony in the Acoma way, the Christian burial in Santa Fe completed with a ceremony to release their spirits in Acoma before sunset. More memories. "One day, this will be yours."

This is what María intended to share with her family tomorrow when all awoke, not the tragedy and sorrow of death, but the legacy of love, of sharing, of blending into a rich and colorful life. The treasure that comes at the end of a job well done.

The White Buffalo Kachina, in all his regal splendors, is merely a symbol of a love that will always exist to those who knew Carlos and Rufina. The legacy of Rainbow.

Elvera Adolfita De Baca

Ben

It was late summer of 1938. Ben was young, strong and good looking. Ben could sing too. He would play the guitar and sing with his happy sounding voice.

Ben was laughter and "chistes." Little jokes about people or things about the community or the times. And everyone was "alegre" when Ben was near. There were also the traditional and familiar that was the Spanish community and Ben's young life. He spoke fluent Spanish. He also spoke English. His English was clear, with a hint of accent.

He said to me. "Vamos avisarle a la gente que regresó tu mama a Nuevo México." I was not sure what he was saying to me, because I did not understand a word of Spanish. But I could tell by the gesture of his out-stretched hand he wanted me to go with him. My mother was in the room with us and she said to me it was "O.K. to go with my brother." To tell you the truth, Ben was not her brother, but her nephew (which is another story) and my "primo hermano." He was thirteen years my senior and I was taught respect as a child, like all the other children, to address our older relatives as "tía" or "tío." So Ben was my uncle. He took me by the hand and we went out into the bright, warm New Mexico October morning.

I was going to be introduced to the happy, little farm community of Pajarito. This was a new world to me and for a small seven year old it became an adventure I will never forget.

Pajarito was not prosperous, like most farming villages of the time. Most of the families struggled day by day to keep food on the table and clothing on their backs. Ben was out of work. Most of the men were. All the farm jobs were taken. Ben worked spasmodically when someone got the news to him soon enough that there was a job to be had, though just for a few days. Sometimes he would be lucky and he would be employed. His pay would be sparse but a few dollars spent wisely helped the family a great deal. The family was very large and always in need. It was a hard time for Ben to be young. But today he would push the troubles to the back of his head somewhere to be forgotten as long as possible, because Fiesta was just a few weeks away and his sister had come back home. Plenty of reason to celebrate.

My small hand was almost lost in his strong hand which was a beautiful shade of brown. Anyone today would be envious of his superb tan but during those depression years it meant he worked hard and long under the hot, ever enduring New Mexico sun.

As we were leaving our grandmother's adobe house, we left by the kitchen door. Everybody took this route, coming or going. It was one of my first impressions of the families and their homes in the small Spanish village. The kitchen was the hub of every family.

Stepping outside into the warm, sunbaked day, we turned towards the back of the house and to the fields. There sitting on the ground, with her back against the outside kitchen wall was my Aunt Rose, my mother's oldest sister. Her hands were a bright crimson, so red they seemed unreal to me. It was the red juice she was working from the dried chili and water she was grinding with a stone in a back and forth motion on the "metate." "Hmmm, the smell of red chili." From then on I knew the smell of red chili. It was on the table every day at every meal. Every household had chili on their table. It would almost be a disgrace if there were no chili! She said to us, "Es muy bueno este chile, me están ardiendo las manos." Ben explained to her, we were taking the back way because we were going to tell the Muñiz first about my mother's return. We would be gone most of the day.

We walked through grandmother's apple orchard and came upon the banks of a narrow irrigation ditch. No water was running in it, Ben said, because the irrigation season was over. There was a path on the other side. We walked over to it on a piece of lumber that had been nailed to the sluice. The path along the ditch would allow only one person to travel on it at a time. Ben let my hand free and said "be careful and do not fall down. It is a very uneven path and in some places the tree roots have made deep ruts." I ran on ahead to see what would lay before me—a long bumpy path, huge old cottonwoods, their leaves yellow, yellow as could be and on either side other orchards and acres of fields now at rest because harvest was over. Coming towards us was a tall, dark man. Ben greeted him. "Hey primo, dónde vas?" Ben greeted all his fellow men as "primo;" everybody else did too. It was a welcome as well as a greeting and everybody was extremely friendly and you were one of them when you were primo, but he was our cousin. Not a close relation but somewhere in line with all the rest of our many cousins. The man's name was Acensión but everyone knew him by the short version of his name, "Chon." "Quién es la muchachita?" he asked. Ben explained to him, as he would do a dozen times or so that day about our arrival and my mother's decision to stay on in Pajarito and make it home. Ben stepped to one side of the narrow ditch path to let Chon by. Chon said, "Voy para tu casa ahora, a dar mis buenos días a Doña Sofía y a ver la Valería." This personal welcome would be made by all family and friends. It was a courtesy to the family and to let my mother know they were happy she had returned to stay.

I continued to run on, enjoying all the delightful new sights and then stopped; before me was a sandy road. Ben reached me. He took my hand again. The road emerged from between the fields and then turned out of sight. I could see one house not far from us. It sat close to the ditch. We did not stop there. Ben said, "that's your Aunt Rose's house." We strolled along the curve of the road, our footprints left in the sand behind us. It was very quiet. No one to be seen anywhere. It was country quiet. The blue sky, completely blue, without a cloud. It encompassed so much. "How could it," I thought, "cover such a big world?"

Ben raised his arm and pointed to the far-off distance, past large alfalfa fields, to some adobe houses almost not visible because they blended with the earth so well. He said, "you can see the ristras de chili hanging from the vigas."

The strings of chili were the same red I had seen on my aunt's hands. And the colorful strings of red chili could be easily seen. "That is the farm of los Muñiz." I noticed Ben's English was mixed with Spanish. "We will visit with them first."

The Muñiz brothers greeted us as we reached their kitchen door. We went into the kitchen and they asked us to sit down. We sat on a wooden bench near a big table. One of the brother's name was Chino and the other Toche, though these were another short version of their real names. Both brothers spoke only Spanish. And Chino said, "Mamá todavía está muy enferma." Ben responded by saying (in Spanish), "I'm sorry to hear your mother is still sick. How are you and Toche getting along?" "As well as can be expected" Chino said. "Have you sold many of the ristras of chili?" asked Ben. "No" said Chino. "I'm going to have to try and sell them in Albuquerque. No one wants to let go of the little money they have." He waved his arm out in a gesture to all about him. "I came to tell you," Ben said, "that Valería is here now." "Sí?" said Chino, like a question. Toche finally spoke out of curiosity. "Vino mi prima de Dember, y cuándo llegó?" "This is her daughter" Ben looked at me. "They arrived a few days ago." "Qué bueno" said Chino. "Explain to Doña Sofía that we may not be able to see her because mother is still sick." Ben said "no te apenes," (not to worry). "God knows what to do. We will go now. We are on our way to Chavez." Chino said "pray for us and our mother."

It was a much shorter route we took to Aurora and Ramón Chávez' farm. Ben took the lead and I followed on an almost invisible foot path through an alfalfa field. The house could not be seen until we were almost upon it because a couple of cottonwoods with low branches kept it from view.

Aurora was home and answered Ben's knock on the screen door. Ben's salutation was "Buenos días le de Dios." She seemed elated to see us and swung the screen door open for us. "Mira quiénes están aquí. Benses cómo has estado? Entren, entren." Her kitchen was bright and flooded with light coming in from three large windows. They held buckets of house plants on the thick, wide adobe window sills.

Ben didn't have a chance to answer her question. She was so surprised and happy to have us as visitors that she hustled about the kitchen busy putting cups on the table and at the same time asking us to sit down by the table. Her eyesight was not very good. She squinted; her small eyes almost closed. And she brought everything she was working with up close to her face to see it better. This didn't seem to hamper her from skittering around the kitchen. And upon her unanswered questions she said "aquí tengo chocolate muy bueno, lo hice con leche fresca. Y tengo biscochitos también."

Ben started laughing and in laughter said "ay Aurora, siéntese con nosotros para poder responder por que estamos aquí." She said in Spanish,

"I know why you are here. Your sister has come back. Little gets by me, I always know what's going on." They both laughed at this.

She poured out hot chocolate into three large cups and then sat down to join us. Their conversation went back and forth, one and then the other, while we drank spicey New Mexican chocolate and ate biscochitos.

The morning was now coming to noontime, and we were on our way again. Back on the sandy road heading for the "Castillos" Ben said. I was eager to find what other new discoveries would be before me. The Castillos' small adobe was nestled back away from Highway 85. It had a large front yard.

They were an elderly couple, their children no longer living with them. Their children were all married with children of their own. Matilde and Teófilo were seldom alone. All their children visited them often. They had great grandchildren too.

The kitchen door was open. And as we walked through the yard towards the house we could hear Doña Matilde calling out loudly to Señor Teófilo (because he was hard of hearing). "Teófilos traime mas leña del cuartito." Then she said out loud to herself, "Qué hombre, no oye nada." She tried once more, much louder this time, "Teófilos! no me oyes?" "Qué quieres mujer?" Teófilo finally heard.

Ben knocked on a much used, wobbly screen door. His knock interrupted her as she was about to make another attempt to reach her husband with strained vocal chords. She walked over to answer the knock on the door. She opened the screen door and was surprised to see Ben and said, "Benses, va qué sopresa, entren. Cómo has estado? Mira quien está aquí Teófilos." Señor Teófilo's hearing was not good but his eyesight was very good. "Benses" he said, "no has venido aquí por muncho tiempo. Cómo has estado?"

We stepped into a large kitchen. It was to me, a pretty one, with white curtains hanging from the windows and wooden cupboards painted the color of the blue sky. The inside ceiling vigas were stained dark. There were no spider webs clinging to them (as I had seen on others before) and they looked as if they just been dusted. The room was filled with the aroma of cooking food. On a large wood burning stove was a large clay pot and inside it bubbling frijoles. In a smaller one red chili was simmering. The large round table had a flowered oilcloth tablecloth on it and there were chairs and benches to sit on. Over the door leading to other rooms was a crucifix, with Jesus crucified on it. A santo I had never seen before, Jesus was painted a stark white with splashed of red paint all over him.

Señor Teófilo wanted to talk to Ben. We sat down at the table. Except Doña Matilde. She said it was time to eat, and started setting the table. Ben introduced me to them. He told them who I was. Some of the Spanish words were becoming familiar to me, but for the most part, I did not know what they were saying. I smiled a lot. I liked them; I liked everyone else I had met that day but they really made me feel at home.

We served fresh cooked frijoles on white porceline dinner plates. Red chile guisado (with meat) was spooned over the beans. Except mine. Tortillas, warm from the top warming oven were placed in the center of the table. They drank coffee and Doña Matilde gave me a glass of milk. We made the sign of the cross before we ate. Lunch lasted a long time. Señor Teófilo had a lot of catching up to do on current events. And Ben didn't mind talking a pitch or two higher for his friend to hear. Doña Matilde asked me if I would like more to eat. I had had my fill but Ben loved his chili and got a second serving. I asked Ben if I could go out and play. Ben then asked Doña Matilde and she said it would be alright because there wasn't anything outside that could hurt me. The visit with the Castillos was rather a lengthy one. When we finally said our goodbyes the children were returning home from school. We were walking back home along Highway 85, the only paved road then in those parts. It is still known as "El Camino Real." Ben pointed to the left of us where there were lots of trees, all cottonwoods. "That is where the river is. You must never go there unless a grownup is with you."

Nearing grandmother's I asked, "what is that wall for?" "That is the Breeze Estate," he said. "It is very big. They also have a few fields. Sometimes I work there but not often."

Ben and I were glad to get home. I gave mother an excited report about all I had seen and done and also said, "we sure do have a lot of cousins." And mother laughed.

There was a steady stream of people who came to visit at my grandmother's for the next couple of weeks. Usually my mother was home to receive them. If not my grandmother, Doña Sofia happily took over the social amenities.

About a week before Fiesta most of the family had gathered one evening at grandmother's house. They were all in the kitchen, of course. It was a small kitchen. The grownups crowded into it. The children, including myself, played in the other rooms. Playing hide n' seek in the bedroom, under and around the beds and furniture. We didn't pay much attention to the grownup conversation. But then we heard music and singing voices. Ben had taken up his guitar and was sitting on the bedroom step leading to the kitchen. His sister Rita was sitting on a chair near him. Rita and Ben were singing a popular song of the time. The voices blended beautifully together to the rollicking, joyful "Jalisco, Jalisco." They sang: "Jalisco, Jalisco tú tienes tu novia que es Guadalajara." All of us loved their singing and music. We stopped our playing and listened. There was clapping and laughter and they were urged to sing more. How long into the night the family celebrated I do not know. I and my other cousins fell asleep all too soon.

I can still hear Ben's guitar, his voice, and he and his sister singing.

María Dolores Gonzales

Respect My Name

You walked into her classroom
with a smile in your eyes
told her your name, Rafael!
she asked if you had another
and you proudly replied, yes
Gonzalo..
"Don't you have a nickname"?
you said NO!
Because she could not
pronounce either one
she renamed you Rafe.
Your big black eyes
filled with anger
and from that day on
for the rest of the year
you stopped listening to her.

Apolonia

Te acuerdas de ese día
cuando decidiste ser
independiente y aventurosa
en los llanos estacados?
No se veía ningún alma
desde la silla
solamente los ojos de los
toros masticando la pastura.
Una casa de adobe abandonada
un par de zapatos
y una revista de
National Geographic.
Te enfrentaste con el
ojo de la cámera oscura
y allí mismo reconociste
a tu abuela, Apolonia.
Le diste una mirada
de confianza que se
reveló en la hoja en
blanco.
Hiciste contacto con todos
los fantasmas de tus
antepasadas.
Cada una de ellas
marchaba con los ojos
pegados hacia el horizonte
listas para luchar
armadas con ese orgullo
de ser hembras que en el
vientre llevaban
los secretos de la vida.

2 de octubre, 1987

Juanita Jaramillo Lavadie

Gramita On The Road

Mom would always hold her breath whenever Grandma Feliz was out visiting relatives. Years before, Grandma and Grampa Ruperto would travel together a lot, so Gramita learned to be comfortable on the road away from Taos. Besides, between the generations, and well tapped into the extended family, there was always someone she knew on the way to stop and visit.

This was fine for a while, even after Grampa Ruperto passed away, but Gramita also comes from a family blessed with longetivity. Gramita, well into her eighties, was still traveling many miles on her family visits, when most of her primas and comadres were anymore content to have the parentela come by and visit them in Taos. With Gramita, we never knew quite what to expect.

Gramita's trip to Los Angeles to visit prima Lucy is still one for the record. Prima Lucy moved to Los Angeles 50 years ago when Tío Lauriano found work as a mechanic. Pues la prima Lucy was going to be at the Los Angeles airport, waiting for 'Mita's arrival at around 3:00 p.m. Tío Ben, Gramita's older brother, and his daughter Marta had taken 'Mita to the airport in Albuquerque that same morning.

The flight exchange was in Bakersfield, and that was where Gramita got off thinking she had "arrived" when she heard the stewardess announce "California" on the intercom. Pero, no había nada de conocidos esperándola allí en el aeropuerto. She waited assuming that prima Lucy might be a little late, but no one showed up.

Realizing that maybe something was wrong, Gramita mustered her best English and went to the airline counter to find out what had happened. After the airline ticket agent finally figured out what happened, 'Mita was on her way to Los Angeles, but only after a number of hours had passed.

Pues, allí en Los Angeles se quedó la prima Lucy en el aeropuerto esperando y esperando. Having Gramita paged several times, prima Lucy thought she had better call Tío Ben in Albuquerque. That's when he got concerned. He called to the airline office in Albuquerque to try to find out what happened to Gramita. Mientras tanto, prima Lucy went back home to wait, con ansias y pena. Tío Ben and his family were very punctual and precise by nature, and if he was surprised, then where was my Gramita?

It was late that night when Gramita called prima Lucy to come and get her at the airport in Los Angeles. Asegurándole que todo estaba bien, and after soothing prima Lucy's jangled nerves, Gramita would laugh about her little adventure in the Bakersfield airport. Well, she did get special care and first class treatment. ¡Cómo que no! Grampa had always catered to her travel tastes anyway, and she was no stranger to travel.

In spite of the ripples this Los Angeles trip had caused in the family, it wasn't as bad as her trip about five years ago. This was after visiting her daughter's family in Utah. Gramita waited for her bus in Salt Lake City, planning to arrive the following day in Albuquerque. There Tío Ben was supposed to meet her at the bus depot about 18 hours after she left Utah.

That was when she thought she heard the departure notice announced and boarded her bus. Making herself comfortable in the bus, she prepared herself for the long drive. It was a couple of hours before she suspected that the bus was not heading south to Albuquerque.

Everyone here in Taos was fine, preparing for Gramita's return home, until Tío Ben called Mom. Grandma was not on the bus, and no one in Salt Lake knew where she was. Her luggage had arrived in Albuquerque, but not Gramita.

Everyone waited and waited, but there was no word of Gramita's whereabouts. Mom was maintaining, but she was really worried. Still, there was no trace of Grandma in Salt Lake, nor in Albuquerque. Finally, nearly 40 hours after she had last been seen, Tío Ben got a phone call from Gramita, who had just arrived at the bus depot in Albuquerque.

Oh, she had a little story of her adventure, but it took a while for everyone else to settle down. She said she had noticed that the bus was taking a different route out of Salt Lake City, but when the unfamiliarity of the road extended into a couple of hours, she asked the bus driver, in her best English, when they were due to arrive in Albuquerque.

The bus Gramita was on was headed for Cheyenne, Wyoming. After looking at her purchased bus ticket, the bus driver realized what had happened and somewhere between Salt Lake City and Denver, saw to it that this little viejita who spoke little English was given special treatment and returned to Salt Lake City. It was arranged through the busline offices for her to head back south to Albuquerque, with careful watch so that she would not make the same mistake. She also made sure that each new bus driver read the printed destination on her ticket.

Mientras tanto, according to Gramita, every available telephone she saw was being used, so she couldn't call home, and once on the bus, she didn't get off unless the bus driver stopped for meals. She didn't want to get lost again. Even during the short meal stops, all the telephone booths were occupied, so she never had a chance to call, but she was okay. She was accommodated so that she could tell us, "Hasta Nueva York podía ir, muy agusto y bien tratada."

Gramita's traveling days are limited now that she is in her nineties. But she still likes to pasear, and always has some stories to tell, like the time she tried to borrow Eduardo's car on Día de los Innocentes; "es que" Mom was going to drive her to Peñasco.

Mary Montaño Army

The Chaos Chronicles

(excerpts)

I suppose the reason I cried most of the way home from the concert is not that the symphony did an encore—it hardly ever does encores—but that the encore was Edward Elgar's Pomp and Circumstance March No. 1. The slow section is the well known graduation march. To me, it's always been more than a march. It's a portrait of my father. It's the essence of what he believed in when he waxed poetic about Humanity and Knowledge and the Universe in General. It's as close to a personal theme song as I can imagine. I cried because I miss him.

When I heard Elgar's music, an image flashed in my mind—that old photograph of my father, taken in the early 50's when he was a college student at the University of New Mexico—José Nestor Montaño. In it, he sits with a casual grace, leaning back in a wooden chair, handsome and smiling like some kind of Hispanic Cary Grant. Papers and books lie on the table in front of him; it's obvious a friend with a camera broke into a study session. In the background, the tall, stately windows of Zimmerman Library's timeless west wing glow with diffused sunlight.

My father was the second person in our family history to get a university degree, if you don't count Padre Vicente S. Montaño of the 19th century, who needed some advanced schooling before they'd let him go traipsing all over New Mexico dispensing religion and education. It was my father's G.I. benefits that got him through six years and two degrees (and before him, my uncle Robert). Without the war, and the benefits, it's unlikely he or my uncle Robert would have gotten that far, but I shouldn't be so sure. His father, Pedro Ignacio Montaño, an Hispano with ancient roots in the Southwest, was a clerk in an Anglo-owned, rural general store in Antonito, Colorado.

His father before him was a rancher. No one paid much attention to books. No one had time.

Padre Montaño, on the other hand, my fourth-great uncle, had the advantage of a mentor. He attended the first school in northern New Mexico at Taos, run by Padre Martínez himself, in his own home. Padre Martínez not only had time for books, he was passionate about them. He wrote and printed his school's textbooks in Taos on his own printing press. Over the years, Padre Martínez sent eighteen of his brightest graduates to the seminary in Durango, Mexico, to continue their studies and become much needed native priests. My great uncle was one of the eighteen. The only document I've uncovered on him so far is a letter he wrote—in the fanciest gentleman's handwriting style of those florid 19th century letter writers—to a Santa Fe power broker, asking for a donation of *vigas*. Padre Montaño had set his mind on repairing the smaller of two churches at Abiquiu, the one for the *genizaros*, or Indian-Hispanic half-breeds. They had their own church because the *sangre puro* crowd wouldn't have them in their own church— the one with the roof.

Why would my father want a degree? Why did he want to teach Spanish, and Spanish Culture to New Mexican students? What was different about Dad that store clerking wasn't enough? Was he following Padre Montaño's lead? Listening to his notions of the purpose of the arts in society gave me a hint. The arts, he said to me, are *the* civilizing element of mankind. They show us that there is more to living, he said, than simply existing. Artists, musicians, dancers and writers point the way for us and show what the human spirit can attain and accomplish. We are not on this earth to simply survive. We're here to leave the world a better place than when we arrived. To make it beautiful, and bearable, with art. Ah? I was breathless when he finished talking. And I wondered where he got such lofty notions. No one else in my circle of family or friends, or fathers of friends, spoke like that. Ever. Nor did they introduce plays by classical Spanish playwrights to the local high school in Antonito. My father directed his students in productions of works by Cervantes, Lope de Vega, Ramón de la Cruz. Nor was that enough. He talked their parents into letting him take their kids, his students, to Mexico, where they saw the real thing. He taught for many years in Albuquerque and must have taken hundreds of young Hispano students to Mexico.

For me, it was enough that he had what may have been one of the only record players in the county when I was growing up. A luxury to most people, it was a necessity to my father and me, as we listened together to Beethoven, Tchaikovsky, Katchaturian and—Elgar. Or that he finally bought a piano when I was 14, even if we couldn't afford lessons and I ended up cleaning another school auditorium in exchange for lessons. Our neighbors and relations—what some would call "good, honest, working folk"—were, I think, in awe of him and maybe suspicious of his ideas. Maybe that's why they treated him with deference while at the same time not entirely accepting him as one of their own. He was "just *different*, you know?"

Nevertheless, that record player, and that music, were unlike anything I'd ever heard before in my short child's career in Antonito. I know, because I had many relatives all over southern Colorado, and they didn't even own radios, let alone record players. I couldn't understand how they managed without music. I'd listen to these joyous, eloquent sounds and then go outside and the shimmering new snow on the ground, or the delicate pink blossoms on the crabapple trees, or the cool summer rain, or the billowing black smoke from the coal train, or the crystalline air of Indian summer in that high mountain valley were all more vivid and alive for me because the music was still resounding in my head and my heart.

When I hear Elgar's march now, I remember my father walking across still another auditorium to receive his graduate diploma at the university commencement exercises. I was about ten years old when he finished his master's degree. I know my father worked very hard for that day. I remember hot summer afternoons in Albuquerque, where we moved when I was six. While we children napped or played, he was bent over his books or sat typing a paper into the night. Then he rose early in the morning to drive a bread truck to support us, his family. He didn't have to go through all this. He could have been a store clerk like Pedro Ignacio. But, no, it wasn't enough.

When I hear Elgar's march now, I think on the next generation—my older cousin Bobby, my younger sister Elizabeth and myself receiving our graduate diplomas from Adams State College, St. John's College, Stanford University, and the University of New Mexico. We make inane, weak jokes about how being college educated city dwellers makes us more than ever like the "cultural *coyotes*" we already knew we were. And how worthless the diplomas often are on the job market—but we've *got* them, and being a cultural *coyote* means being a bridge to the rest of the world. And those diplomas are an accomplishment not only for ourselves, but for everyone else back in Antonito, and for Padre Montaño, who wouldn't want to be alone in his efforts. He might even laugh and say it's about time our family learned to reach out to the world and soak up knowledge and the arts for their own sake, job or no job.

I had a nightmare last night and in my dream, I fled to my father's room after the fright had occurred, and he was there, and he comforted me with a kind, compassionate voice, so full of love and understanding. To calm me down, he showed me the book he was currently reading. Judging from it's thickness, it was at least a thousand pages long, and its title was "The Characters of Men." At the time I said to myself, this is a typical book for him to be reading—a huge study of the courage and fortitude of the human spirit. In the dream, he asked me how my own writing projects were going. We discussed them in detail. In time, I forgot the fright that had driven me to his room. I was comforted by his loving presence and his interest in my work.

Then I woke up. That day I hovered in a warm serenity, because even though my father had been dead for seven years, I knew he was still watching over me. And my education.

Gina Montoya

An Open Good-Bye Letter To My Son

I

He was seventeen
when his father took him
to Las Cruces

NEW MEXICO STATE UNIVERSITY

To check out the new college,
he would go to in the Fall of 1987
He would go out into the world.

"Move away from home, Move away from
your mother," said his father.
Become independent, so it won't be too
easy on you" (Well, it never was so
easy being a family, the two of us
          alone for fiteen years, Never)
A single mother, a lone child,
living together, the two of us
               against time,
               against the world.
Your father can never break the umbilical
chain which will shriek in the wind,
                         on the sea,

                    yet free.

II

The day I thought about my son's leaving
My emotions felt and my heart heard
 the cat wallow
 the dog howl
 the wind growl
 the mother's heart empty
      along with the house
       your room
       your presence
        music different.

The mingled joy and sadness
of the voices of our mixed races
you "coyote" the hope of neutrality
the hope of wiping out racism.
Carry hope with you always.

III

Remember. You are a son of a feminist/humanist
within our culture, within our religion.
Remember as you fly from the nest, little bird
to beat your wings in rebellion for the
   truth you will be seeking.

IV

I wish you dreams of high flight,
and the chirp of a new song/melody.

Live the fire of enthusiasm
Light your eyes with true martyr spirit
Allow it to burn in your heart and soul.

For Jerry Reeder, September, 1987

Juanita M. Sánchez

Ciprianita

lita who spoke to the wild
    brought to the river
crickets and their songs
    brought to the river her drum
and the sound of a cat's paw
    beating on my chest

lita
    i wish i could have been with you
in those years when there were no weapons
    that would cause giant mushrooms
on the earth and scars on the faces of the east
    erupting, later, in the hearts of the children

how hateful the times of my years
    my witness to these politics
systems of money above need
    yet
lita
    was it really any better when you were growing,
speaking only spanish, then as a widow
    you had three children to raise
in the united states?

but you had it all
    your oil lamps, metate, flowered apron
and the clothes line with your hanging corn,
    carne seca, red chile
chile so hot our ears burned

remember, lita, when i went with you to sears
    to help you find a dress with pockets
it had to have pockets
    little bolsitas to hold your cigarettes
and leather snap-together coin purse
    remember, lita, we were both afraid of the escalator
the moving stairs made us dizzy
    we weren't ready for high-tech then...
oh then, when we were driving home
    us kids in the back seat of the '48 olds
you pulled out bags of chip potatoes
    we thought you were so rich
to give us each a bag
    and i loved playing with the hairs under your chin
you said god gave them to you, so why pull them out

lita
    you died too soon
fifty-five year old grandmother
    telling us stories in spanish
that kept us awake all night
    not because they were long
but because they were scary
    i never could sleep in your house
with all the fear i had
    of the ghosts that visited you
the hand of my young dead cousin knocking
    on your bed post and crawling toward your pillow

one time
    when i put paint on my face
you told me that my skin was going to fall off
    and i'd wake up a skeleton
puro huesos y nada más que huesos
    i couldn't sleep because i kept touching my face and hands
to make sure the skin was still there

lita
    you died too soon
remember the pact you made with my mother
    you told her that you would teach me spanish
and she would teach me english
      i learned your language
but you left me too much in the hands
    of the gringo schools
they didn't like what you taught me
    they made me over
it hurt, lita, it hurt so bad
    but i promised you, lita
i promised to remember all you told me
    even the scary stories and sleepless nights
that i would pass them on
    and you could live forever

lita
    you did speak to the wild
i can still hear the songs you whistled
    still smell the tortillas on the iron stove
still taste the ground chile on the stone
    hey lita!
i can speak spanish real good now
    ¡oígame lita!
es tu idioma, ¿recuerdas?
    ¡lita!
i feel the cat on my chest again
    your drum   i imagine

Linda Sandoval

A Short Trip Home

"Boy, sure was a long ride on that crummy bus," Sara said as she plopped her duffle bag alongside her brother Jacob's beat-up suitcase.

It was hot and humid, even though the sun was retiring for the day. The traffic didn't notice the sunlight's departure as it continued its loud humming. There were many passengers milling about, unloading their suitcases from the dingy and stuffy vehicle now parked at the bus station. The two-hour ride had taken its toll on everyone because to Jacob they looked drained and lacked energy.

"I'm tired," mumbled Sara. She sat side-saddle on Jacob's suitcase and began gnawing at her thumbnail.

"Yeah, me too," Jacob answered wearily. "Let's get a Coke or something, O.K.?"

He quickly reached into the inner pocket of his jacket and heard the familiar sound of crackling paper as his hand groped for his wallet. Pulling the paper out, he noticed that it was an envelope. He thought it was the utility bill their dad had asked him to pay earlier that week. Unfolding the envelope, he noticed his name on the front.

"Come on, Jake," Sara moaned. "Let's go inside and get something to drink—I'm dying of thirst."

"Hold on," Jacob said, anxiously tearing the envelope open.

"I'm going on ahead, slowpoke," Sara said over her shoulder as she walked toward the bus station's entrance.

When Jacob looked closer, he recognized the scrawled letters of his dad's handwriting and began reading:

> Dear Jacob
> It so hard for me to say this to you in purson
> espeshally after the arguemint we had last nite.
> It was not rite that I yelled and pushed you. I
> am sorry. awnest.I just get carryed away
> sometime and I get mad too much. I will try
> to lissen more to you when you talk. Studdy hard
> in class today o.k.
> Dad

Jacob stared at the letter, his mind racing with thoughts that fit together like a jigsaw puzzle: no wonder Dad didn't get the promotion at the welding shop, he thought. How can he read the blueprints if he can't write well? That's probably why he acted the way he did last night.

It seemed as though Sara had never left, since she was standing behind Jacob when he turned around.

"Want a drink?" she asked, smiling. Her smile was slowly erased by Jacob's silence. He couldn't answer because his throat hurt and his eyes were crowded with tears.

"Jake, are you O.K.?" Sara asked worriedly.

"Yeah, yeah," mumbled Jacob, trying to control the trembling of his voice. He quickly wiped his face with the palm of his hand, then stuffed the letter into the pocket of his jacket.

"Hey, why don't we go inside and check when the next bus leaves back to Oakview, O.K.?" he suggested, putting his arm around her. "I'll bet Dad won't even notice we were gone, since it's his bowling night, and I'll bet we could get a late dinner started in no time flat—pizza, maybe—what do you say?"

"But I thought we were running away from home, Jake," Sara said, scratching her head in confusion. "I thought we were both tired of Dad's grouchy ways. I mean, ever since Mom died two years ago, he doesn't act the same."

"I know, I know," Jacob admitted. "Let's just try to stick together, O.K.? I mean, Dad needs us."

On the way back to Oakview, they talked and talked. To Jacob it was the shortest ride home.

Nell Soto Sehestedt

Private Views

"Is that you sneezing again, Eduardo?"

The young man stifled another sneeze just before Rogelia appeared at the door of his room, a worried frown on her face.

"I think you're coming down with something. You're run down from working so hard my son."

"Mamá, I've told you over and over. It's an allergy, not a cold. I sneeze because of the pollen in the air."

"Allergy, hmmph," she muttered. "It certainly sounds like a cold. And you know that you've lost weight, Eddie. I bet you're not eating any lunch at work." As usual they spoke in Spanish.

"Of course I have lunch. Don't start that."

"I wish you'd let me fix you a good lunch every day."

Eddie tried to control the irritation in his voice. "I'd rather eat a hot meal in the cafeteria than a cold sandwich from a paper sack. But, thanks anyway, Mamá. Now I have to hurry." He crowded past her into the bathroom, where he ran the shower in a great torrent.

Still annoyed by his mother's importuning, Eddie dressed quickly. He grabbed the briefcase in one hand and his jacket in the other, pausing only to peck at Rogelia's cheek in his customary leave-taking.

"My son, take plenty of handkerchiefs with you," she called as he raced for the car.

Getting into traffic distracted him temporarily, but once he was on the smoothly flowing freeway, he vented his ire with vehement thoughts. "How can your own mother, someone you love, irritate the hell out of you?" he wondered. "Why does she cluck around and set your nerves on edge

89

every single day?"

Eddie gripped the steering wheel as though he could squeeze an answer out of it. He told himself, "You're a reasonably sensible, organized-type guy, right? You handle the money at home and you keep up with world events. So why does your mother think she has to spoon-feed you and lay out your underwear every morning?"

He recalled hearing her admonitions since the age of five, and a familiar wave of vexations swept over him. "Eat all your breakfast, Eddie. Wear a sweater today." As the years passed, it was "Study, my boy. Read more. Work harder." Her words had become embedded in his brain through repetition.

The young man turned onto the off ramp leading to his workplace in reflex action, because his mother's words occupied his mind. "And here you are." Eddie summarized his situation, "28 years old and she's still harping about the same things!"

He drove into the company parking lot, his skin prickly with resentment. He stalked into his office, unaware of the frown on his face. A clerk and a junior accountant who saw it, exchanged glances of warning.

Meanwhile, Rogelia had remained at the back porch where she had waved good-bye, leaning her short, stout form on a corner post.

"Muchacho burro!" she breathed with some heat. "Never pays attention to what I say. Always in a big hurry. but if you get sick, tonto, who has to worry and take care of you, eh?" She watched until Eddie's car was out of sight, her eyes and mouth tightened into lines of displeasure.

* * *

The sun slanted brightly through the shutters into Anita's kitchen. She hummed as she finished the chores after breakfast and after getting her husband off to work. Anita looked forward to a leisurely chat with her friend and neighbor.

"Buenos días, Rogelia."

"Hola, Anita, how are you? Kids off to school yet?"

Yes, they just got on the bus. The little one was cranky already. Ah, it's good to have a few hours of quiet around here."

Rogelia laughed. "I remember when my Eduardo was that age. He'd complain about getting up, but I never let him miss school unless he was sick."

"You say he went to college?"

"Oh, yes, Anita. He graduated," Rogelia underlined proudly. "He finished four years of college. That was before you moved into the neighborhood."

"You're lucky he's such a responsible young man. So neat and quiet," Anita stated. "But these kids of mine, they argue all day long. The big one likes to study, thank God."

"That's good. Keep afer them, my dear. Listen, you don't know the sacrifices I made to keep Eddie in college. I worked ten hours a day in that miserable sewing factory so we could eat and pay for his books. Once in a while I have to remind him of all that."

"Holy Virgen," Anita said softly. "But Rogelia, you're so set on education, how come you dropped out of high school?"

Rogelia heaved a deep sigh. "That's my biggest regret, Anita. I quit school to get a job and help out at home."

"There are adult classes if you want to get a diploma," her friend reminded her.

"Yes, I know. But Eddie needs me here at home. And besides, I feel self-conscious with strangers."

"Nonsense, Rogelia. That's just an excuse to do nothing."

Rogelia became uncomfortable with the truth thus presented. "Perhaps so. One of these days I may get the courage to enroll in a class for tontas like me. Well, I have to go, now. Hasta luego, Anita."

Already lost in thought, Anita replaced the receiver and picked up a wet mop. She began to swab the kitchen floor slowly, in pace with her musing.

"That Rogelia really amazes me sometimes," she averred. "So wrapped up in that son of hers she can't talk of anything else. Willing to do anything for Eddie's good. My God, I know I could never be that devoted to my kids."

She shook her head with a sad smile. "But then, I don't have a good-looking model son like Eddie either."

Anita stopped, rinsed the mop and continued swabbing the floor with long careful strokes.

* * *

"Hey, Lars. What's new, buddy?" Eddie spotted Lars at the cafeteria and hailed his good friend.

"Not much, Ed. Coffee's strong for a change. Grab a cup and tell me what's happening."

"Aw, hell, Lars. Same old crap." Eddie filled a mug and returned to sit by Lars. The latter was a kindly avuncular figure to Eddie, and he had often counselled the younger man.

"Your unit running okay? Any glitches with the software?"

"Smooth so far," Edie replied, but without interest.

"Same here. But I hear that our pal Howard, Unit 6, has run into snags."

Eddie shrugged. "It happens. New programs."

"You look down, Eddie. What's bugging you? If it's not the job it must be your love life, hmmm?"

"Ha, I wish."

"Trouble at home, then?" Lars was aware of the state of affairs with regard to Eddie's mother.

"Yeah, again."

"A case of too much mothering, I guess."

"No, it's more like smothering,"Eddie grumbled. "She doesn't leave me any room to breathe."

"She loves you, Ed, you know that. She doesn't realize she's being over-protective." Lars' large face showed sympathy.

"Sure, I know all that. But how can I make her lighten up? I've tried talking to her. She fusses over me like I'm a snotty little kid going to grammar school." Eddie threw his hands up.

Lars smiled and listened patiently.

"Do you know that I can't keep any beer in the house because she's afraid I'll become a wino, for God's sake?" Eddie griped. " Sometimes I want to yell, 'Can't you leave me alone?' "

"Maybe you should explain all this, but gently, Eddie," Lars now suggested in a serious tone. "Sure, mothers can get carried away and start henpecking."

"She expects too much out of me. She wants me to succeed so much she can taste it," Eddie sighed. "She says maybe I'll own this company someday." He gave a harsh laugh.

"That's not impossible, my friend."

"Come down to earth, man." Eddie discarded the notion with a gesture of his hand.

"Well, have you thought of all the alternatives you have?"

"Such as?"

"Such as you could get your own apartment. You could continue to help your mother financially as you're now doing," his friend pointed out.

"Cheez, that would be a drastic move, Lars. I don't know if I can really leave my mother alone. Abandon her."

"Do you see it as abandonment to get your own place?"

"Lars, I'm all the family she has left. How would she explain to her friends that her son chose to get out of her house, that he no longer wanted to live with her? It would be a humiliation for her."

"I see." Lars looked down at his hands and thought for a moment. "But what if you meet a girl that you want to marry. You'd want your own home then, wouldn't you?"

"Sure. But even if I got married, Mamá would be somewhere in the picture. Maybe in the same house." With set face, Eddie went on grimly. "Damn, at my age most guys are settled, raising their kids, or they're divorced and catting around again. But here I am, still stuck at home, wondering if I'll ever have a life of my own."

Lars gave Eddie a pat on the back as he rose to leave, but he refrained from further comment.

* * *

Eddie called out as he entered the house, "Mamá, I'm home." He threw the briefcase on a chair and loosened his tie. Rogelia hurried into the living room to greet him.

"I'm glad you're back safely, Eddie. Were you busy today? Tell me what you did." She waited expectantly.

"Aw, Ma, I'm tired. It's hot."

"Just tell me what happened at work today, Eddie. I'm here alone all day. I don't have an interesting job like yours, you know."

"All right. At dinner I'll tell you what I did today. But now, let me get out of these clothes so I can relax."

His mother threw him a dark look as she went into the kitchen.

In his room, Eddie shook his head in wonder at the vicarious pleasure his mother took in his activities. "She still wants to hear everything I do each day. Like during college. Every day, the confessional hour."

Rogelia set heaping plates of hot food on the table while she waited for Eddie. As soon as he walked in, she prompted, "Now, what did you do today?"

Eddie took a small helping of roast and vegetables. "Let me see. First I went to a meeting with three other supervisors of the computer units. That took most of the morning."

Rogelia's eyes were shining. "Ah, it must have been important, eh? Why don't you have more squash, Eddie? I baked it the way you like it."

He waved it away. "We talked about short-term depreciation for some of the department's assets."

"Oh, my," breathed Rogelia. "And then?"

"In the afternoon I had to catch up with my regular work." Her son had been vague by intention. "Now what's new here at home? Were you busy?" Eddie ate while he listened.

"Oh, after the housework I watered the yard, and I cut some flowers for the front room."

The meal proceeded in silence for a few minutes. Rogelia was still relishing the important-sounding duties of her son. "Meetings with other supervisors, imagine," she said softly. "I knew you'd amount to something, Eddie." Her glance was full of pride for him.

"Good supper, Mamá. I'll help you clear the table."

Rogelia emerged from her fog. "Why thank you, my son. Of course, I don't understand much of what you say, but it's so good to hear that you——"

She broke off because Eddie had left the room and was rinsing plates at the sink.

* * *

"Hola, Rogelia. How are you today? It's such a beautiful morning I had to get out and work in the garden." Anita's cheerful voice greeted Rogelia on the telephone.

"Yes, Anita, it's lovely today. A little windy, though. The trees are losing their leaves and the wind scatters them all over the yard. Ah, me. No end to work, inside and out."

"Oh, Rogelia, you have a big strong son to do the yard work," Anita teased her friend. "Let Eddie mow the lawn this weekend and rake the leaves. You do enough in the house."

"Actually I don't like to see Eddie doing all that by himself, Anita. He's not too strong and I worry about him. Lately he's been sneezing again——"

"Look, Rogelia, I know you worship the lad, but it won't hurt him to help you with the heavy yard work."

"No, no. I can manage. Besides, I think he's overworked. He has to supervise so many people, lots of paperwork."

"Say, Rogelia, now that Eddie has this fabulous job, why don't you get out and enjoy yourself a little?"

"What could I do at my age? Tell me,"

"You could come with me to the Latinos Social Club. We have good speakers at the luncheons. Dances once in a while. You'd meet people, Rogelia. Nice men."

"Oh, I don't have time for all that. Anita, you don't understand that I have to keep after Eddie. To help him all the time."

"Come on, Rogelia. He's a grown man."

"He has so much reponsibility now that sometimes he's a little insecure. A mother knows these things, Anita. He needs someone to give him confidence. I want to make him a success."

Anita sighed. "I think you've done your part, lady. You have to think of yourself once in a while. What are you going to do when he leaves home?"

"Leave home?" Rogelia was startled. "Why would he want to leave home?"

"My goodness, he'll get married one of these days and go off. Haven't you thought of that, woman?"

Rogelia had become slightly nettled by them. "I suppose so. Just look at the time! I have to go, Anita."

"Hmmm, yes. But think over what I said."

"I will, Anita, and good-bye for now."

* * *

Eddie arrived home from work to find his mother sitting at the kitchen table, her chin cupped in her hand, and staring into space. Usually by this time Rogelia was busy stirring a pan or chopping vegetables, with dinner well underway.

"Hola, Mamá," he greeted her cautiously. "Something wrong?"

She raised a wan face. "No, my son. You're home early."

"Same time as always. You look tired, Mamá. I bet you were pulling weeds all day."

"No, in fact I was lying down all afternoon. I just didn't feel like doing anything." She sighed. "Just getting old and lazy, I guess." She rose to wash her hands at the sink. "I'll have supper ready in a few minutes."

Eddie saw dark circles around her eyes and he watched her move heavily across the room. Putting his arm around her shoulders, he urged, "Tell you what, vieja. Let's eat out for a change. Get your coat."

"Well, I won't argue about that," Rogelia smiled.

While he drove to the restaurant Eddie suggested, "It's been over a year since you had a good physical check-up, Mamá. Why don't you call your doctor and make an appointment?"

With a shrug, Rogelia agreed. "If you say so, my son."

"Yes, call first thing tomorrow for an appointment as soon as possible."

Rogelia merely nodded.

"Oh, and another thing, Mamá, don't iron my jeans, okay?"

* * *

Slowly the door opened, and Eddie looked up from his desk. A young brunette entered, looked about with an uncertain air, then stood before him.

"Mr. Trejo? I'm Olivia Romero. The women in Personnel sent me to talk to you about the job in Accounting."

"Yes, Miss Romero. Please sit down."

The woman perched on the chair, ill at ease, and began to rub her hands. Eddie swept a swift glance over her to get a general impression. Her dress was appropriate, her makeup unobtrusive. She had an oval face with regular features, framed by long wavy hair. Despite her tension, Eddie noted that she was attractive.

"Just relax, Miss Romero. Trejo studied her rèsumé. I see you graduated from Community College with a business major. Good. Is your math your strong point?"

"It was my favorite subject. I like to work with figures." She twisted a handkerchief in her hands.

"And you list two former employers. Total of four years experience in accounting. You were laid off your last job?"

"Yeah. The company closed a couple of stores and I was laid off." Olivia was staring at Eddie in wide-eyed apprehension. Eddie saw that her eyes were a pale amber, the color of warm honey.

He asked, "Do you mind if I use your first name." When she shook her head he went on, "Supposing we hired you, Olivia, and your last employer asked you to return to your old job. Would you go back?"

With a burst of determination she stated, "No, I wouldn't. I'm not waiting to be called back by that outfit. If you give me a job, I'll stick with it." Her face showed such resolve that Eddie smiled.

"Fine," was his comment. He was ready to move on to another subject, but Olivia added, "There was a lot of friction at the last place. One guy was a real agitator. He kept everybody stirred up with his claims of discrimination."

Eddie became interested. "What kind of claims?"

"He said that the Latino employees were being passed over for promotion, getting less pay, stuff like that."

"And did you see signs of discrimination?"

Olivia shrugged. "No, I don't think so. And I never joined the union because I don't like to go to meetings where they talk about strikes and pickets. Always complaining about working conditions. I don't go along with all that."

"Really?" Eddie was puzzled by her indifference.

"I guess it's okay for those guys who are always on the warpath. Not for me."

"Are you Chicana, Olivia?"

The young woman appraised him quickly, trying to decide if he was trying to "offend" her or not. She remained silent.

"As for myself, Olivia, I am Chicano. A Mexican-American. I like to speak Spanish at home." He smiled. "And I'm always glad to see another *paisana* around here."

Olivia defrosted slightly, offering a small smile. "I speak a little Spanish, too. I'm part Italian," she declared. "My parents are Mexican, but my grandmother was part Italian."

Eddie nodded. "No use pursuing that," he thought wearily and turned again to her rèsumé. "We think you would fit well in our department, Olivia. Can you start next Monday at eight in the morning?"

The girl gave a little gasp. "Oh, yes, I can! Thank you Mr. Trejo. You won't be sorry, I promise."

Eddie rose and extended his hand in ritual dismissal. After Olivia left, he reviewed their conversation and her application. "Her work background checked out okay. She's uptight about being a Chicana," he thought. "A hairy burden to put on one's own back. What a shame."

Then he tackled his paperwork.

* * *

A week later Eddie happened to see Olivia as she entered the parking lot at work. He walked over to where she was busy locking both doors of the compact car.

"Good morning, Olivia. I'm glad to see you're a cautious person."

Surprised, she turned a blank stare on him until she recognized him. "Mr. Trejo. You mean about locking doors? Well, this is the first car I've ever owned, and I want to keep it awhile."

Eddie pointed to his own much older vehicle. "There's the first car I ever had and I still lock it."

Olivia laughed with him, and as they walked to the entrance of the building, Eddie asked, "How's the work going so far? Any problems?"

"Oh, not bad. The machines are a little different from my last job, but I'm catching on."

"Sure. Give yourself time. And let me know if I can help."

Olivia flashed him a bright smile that displayed her lovely teeth and pale eyes circled with black lashes. Dazzled, Eddie waved his hand as they parted in the hall.

All morning the brilliant smile and honey-colored eyes haunted Eddie. He saw them everywhere, on each piece of paper he tried to read.

"Watch it," he warned himself. "She's cute stuff, all right, but don't go overboard. All you know about her is her work record. *And* that she has a hang-up about being Chicana." he thought it over. "That's such a destructive attitude. A sign of low self-esteem."

With impatience he pushed her image away and tried to concentrate on the stack of work before him. It was no use. "Hell," he determined at last, "why don't you talk to the girl; try to instill some pride in her heritage? Who knows what drives a person to hide his roots?"

Olivia agreed quickly to have dinner with him that same evening. Back in his office, Eddie reached for the phone and dialed home.

Rogelia answered promptly. "Ah, my son," her voice rang with gladness to hear from Eddie. "Are you calling to remind me again about the doctor's appointment? It's not till next week."

"I know that, Mamá. Be sure to tell him you don't have any pep, and you want a thorough exam."

"I will, Eddie. But he'll probably say that it's because I'm carrying a lot of years on my joroba," she chuckled, "and charge me double for the compliment."

Eddie laughed half-heartedly at his mother's sally, then mustered his courage to state, "Mamá, I won't be home for dinner today."

"Oh," her voice fell with disappointment. "Have you got too much work to do, my son?"

"No, it isn't that."

"But when will you eat? Shall I keep your supper warm?"

"No, please don't. I'll have dinner here in town."

Rogelia was silent for a moment. "With whom, Eddie?"

"With a friend."

"Bueno, can't you tell me the name?"

Eddie's tone was cool. "You don't know the person."

"It's a woman, eh?" Rogelia asked in a near-whisper.

"Yes." He did not volunteer any information, and the rest of the day he felt like a faithless deceiver.

* * *

Dinner had gone smoothly with polite small talk about the job. Now over a brandy, Eddie asked Olivia, "You mentioned your parents at our first interview. What part of Mexico are they from?'

"Ahmm," her eyes opened to a roundness, and Eddie was struck again by their beautiful color. "They're from Morelia. But they came here thirty years ago, and the're U.S. citizens now. My mother's family was part French." She sipped the drink with obvious uneasiness.

"Yes." Eddie toyed with the silverware on the table. Noting the new nationality claimed by the girl, he decided to broach the subject he had in mind.

"As you know, Olivia, there has always been prejudice in this country against us Latinos, mainly because we're 'different' in appearance and culture. Well, this racism has made some Latinos become defensive about our ancestry. Those who feel it's a handicap try to hide it under false flags."

Olivia stirred uncomfortably, but Eddie went on. "Trying to hide what we are is wrong. It boils down to a denial of our own identity, and that can provoke guilt in us." He paused for effect.

"The pity is that many Chicanos know little about our culture or our history as Mexican-Americans. How can a person appreciate his heritage if he knows nothing about it?" he asked.

Suddenly aware that his speech had become stilted, Eddie laughed. "Listen to me, I'm on a soapbox again!"

Olivia, who was confused with his change of roles, did not laugh. "I never thought about any of this before, Mr. Trejo."

"Each of us has to face the reality of who he is, sooner or later. Do you want to know anything about Chicano history, Olivia?"

The young woman shrugged. "I suppose so."

"Tell you what, I'll lend you a book to introduce you gradually to the subject, okay?"

Olivia felt compelled to accept, so she nodded.

"I'll bring it in tomorrow," Eddie promised. "I think you'll enjoy discovering your background."

The evening ended on that scholarly note. As he drove home, Eddie felt little satisfaction in having made the young lady focus her attention on the Chicano experience, if only for a few minutes. On balance, he was disillusioned.

"How can a Chicana go through her entire life without any interest in those things that are of vital importance to her: working conditions at her job, the history of her people, her roots?" he fumed. "How can she be so goddamned shallow, so immature?"

Alone in her apartment that night, Olivia raged while she prepared for bed. "What a total waste! What's with this guy Trejo anyway? I thought we had something going when he asks me for a date. A hunk like him, and a big shot, too. But what happens? Dullsville! He gives me a damned lecture on Chicanos or something. Preaches a sermon, wants me to study!"

She flung her robe on a chair in a fury, then changed to a nightgown. "The nerve of this Trejo, talking to me like he was a some big professor and I'm Dopey Dora."

Olivia threw herself onto the bed and continued to seethe with indignation. "To top it all, I have to read some book of his. On my own time, I suppose!"

She tossed about for a time unable to relax. "Now I remember," she exclaimed. "Somebody at work told me Trejo was a 'Mama's Boy.' Why didn't I listen? I coulda saved myself three hours of boredom!"

Rogelia was watching a late news program when Eddie returned. She shut the set off, saying, "Eduardo, come sit here for a few minutes."

With reluctance, the young man sat beside her.

"Mira, Eddie, I know you want to go out with girls. It's natural. You can talk to me about your lady friend. What's she like? She must be pretty, eh?

Eddie shrugged.

"You didn't tell me her name. Where did you meet her?"

"It's late, 'ma. Can't we talk about it tomorrow?"

"I only want to know when you met this girl. Is she a Latina?"

"Yes, yes. She's a Chicana from work. but she's ashamed of it, and that bothers me. I was trying to talk some sense into her tonight." Eddie's annoyance with Olivia was being compounded by Rogelia's prying.

"I hope you're not still arguing with everybody about discrimination and all that! I remember you talked at a rally at the university that turned into a riot, and you nearly got arrested." Rogelia's face was red with agitation.

"I wasn't arguing with anybody," Eddie muttered.

"If you get people all excited about injustice and those things, you'll just get in trouble, Eddie. You have to think about your job."

"Oh, for Pete's—." He stopped and said with a forced calm, "I'm not a wild-eyed radical, Mamá. What I have to say isn't against the law. And now, I'm tired, so I'll say goodnight." He kissed her cheek, and walked away.

"Are you going out with this girl again, my son?"

"I haven't decided. Buenas noches," he called.

"Buenas noches, Eddie," Rogelia murmured. She sat in the dark for a time, thinking things over. "I hope he doesn't get involved with some chippy and then neglects his work. I have to keep my eye on that boy."

* * *

Lars ran into Eddie, who was drumming his fingers at the supply counter, a few days later. "You look upset, Eddie," he remarked.

"Lars, I've got to talk to you. I'm about to blow a gasket!"

"Come on, guy, settle down," Lars soothed him. "What happened? Is something wrong at work or home?"

"The usual. My mother's bugging me worse that ever. Her constant fussing over me gets me so worked up I can't think straight. Always hovering around, asking questions."

Lars smiled with amused compassion.

"She makes a big deal if I discuss simple human rights with anybody because she's afraid I'll rock the boat and lose my job!" Eddie wiped his forehead. "She starts prying if I look at a girl——."

"You told me your older brother died when you were kids," Lars interjected. "It figures that she centers all her concern on you."

Eddie frowned. "Yeah. But why does she lay a guilt trip on me."

Lars waved his hand. "Hold it. I'm no shrink, so let's get practical. What I suggest is that you get her into a social club where she can find a boy friend. Or have her join an arts and crafts class. This would ease the pressure on you."

"Believe me, I've tried, Lars. She makes excuses."

"Keep trying, and be patient with her," his friend urged. He checked his watch. "Hey, I gotta go back to my cave, Eddie. Hang in there." and he was gone.

Eddie wandered back to his office deep in dejection.

Lars' assistant had been waiting for him. The moment Lars returned to his office, Rob sauntered in with a sheaf of blue print-outs in his hand. He was a beefy young fellow who wheezed with every breath.

"Is that crybaby still whining about his Mommy?" he sneered with a nod in Eddie's direction.

"Cut it out," Lars warned. "That guy's got problems. To him they're big problems, and he doesn't need any more grief from you."

"Some problems, hell!" Rob huffed, but he heeded the signal from his boss and dropped the subject.

* * *

Rogelia picked up the telephone on the second ring. "Anita," she asked after the greetings, "how was the baptism of your nephew last Sunday?" She listened to her friend's report of the elaborate party held after the church ceremony, all the while nodding and murmuring, "Sí, sí."

With an eye on the clock, Rogelia finally broke into Anita's stream of talk. "Mira, Anita, I'm expecting a call from my doctor. I went for a complete examination this morning and he said he would tell me the results of the tests this afternoon. So I better let you go. I'm glad you had a good time, chica. Say 'hello' to your husband for me." She hung up before Anita could launch another conversation.

When Eddie arrived that evening, Rogelia relayed the disquieting news that the doctor had discovered a lump on her breast.

Eddie was alarmed. "Exactly what did he say, Mamá?" Do you need an operation or what?"

"The nurse said something about that, but I don't remember. She said they'll let me know if it's a bad tumor."

"Mamá, try to remember. It's important." His face was colorless.

"Well, let me think."

"I'll call the doctor's office and find out." Eddie reached for the telephone.

"All right, Eddie. Here's the number, but the office is closed now."

Her son dialed and left a message with the answering service. In his head pounded the certainty, "I know it's cancer of the breast. Common among women her age. Good God, that could kill her! But I mustn't frighten her. Please let the doctor return my call soon."

He returned to press Rogelia on the matter. "Try to think what else they told you," he urged.

His mother searched her memory for the doctor's exact words. After a time she lost interest in the task. "Goodness, it's late. I've got to start dinner my son." She hurried into the kitchen.

In a daze Eddie wandered into his room. He felt weak and sat down, thinking, "How can this be—my mother with cancer? That's a fatal disease. What am I going to do?" He groaned, "never to see her again. To come home and not find her here. How could this happen to me."

Suddenly he clutched his head as he remembered. "Oh, no, all those things I said to Lars! How could I run off at the mouth like that about my own mother?"

Eddie looked up and faced the mirror. "You miserable creep," he reviled his image, "crying and complaining about every chicken-shit piddle you could think of, making Mamá sound like a neurotic old witch. And here she's dying of cancer!" He ached with remorse.

"Dear God," he whispered with fervor, "let her live a little longer. Give her a few more weeks, months. Please. I'll make sure she's to the end."

At that moment the telephone rang and Eddie jumped in near panic. He ran to grab the receiver. "Doctor," he gasped, "I'm Mrs. Trejo's son. Can you give me the result of the biopsy?"

As he listened, his face brightened. "Benign. And a mild case of anemia? Iron tablets. Oh, thank God! Yes, yes, doctor, next Thursday at ten. She'll be there." He fairly sang with relief, and hung up.

"No operation necessary! You have a little tumor and anemia, Mamá." he laughed. "Nothing serious, my dear, precious Mamá. All you need are some iron pills." He embraced the bewildered woman and waltzed her around the room.

* * *

The sun was bright on the foliage that rustled in the breeze. Rogelia inhaled the morning air while standing at the back porch. She looked over her flower garden, and as was her custom, she waited to see her son off to work.

Eddie emerged from the house, gave her a real kiss on the forehead and a hug on his way to the carport. Rogelia's eyes were on him every step of the way.

"Your shoe lace is undone. Tie it before you fall on it," she called loudly, adding "tonto" under her breath.

Eddie waved goodbye and drove away, shaking his head. In a few minutes he began to chuckle softly.

"There, your prayers have been answered in full, Eduardo. Everything's back to normal. You better face it chum. Mamá will always see you as a kid, even when she's hassling you about your duties as an adult."

He pondered the point. "Well, what did you expect? You didn't pray that she would change, only that she live!" He smiled in acknowledgement. "Yeah, and you promised that she'd be happy if she were spared. So let's take her to dinner and a movie next week. She loves those melodramatic Mexican films about the Revolution."

Eddie paused for a moment, then laughed aloud with real joy. "As a matter of fact, you do too, cabrón!"

Yolanda M. Troncoso

Toolbox

My father's toolbox is heavy and grey.
It sits on the unfinished floor of his house.
With effort, I can lift out the greasy top shelf.
Screwdrivers with translucent handles sit on wrenches and pliers.
Wooden handled hammers for carpentry lie next to peen-ball
hammers for beating metal into shape.
Nestled protectively in the lift-out shelf are micrometers,
rulers, and calipers.

One Christmas, he gives my little sister a toolbox just like his.
It's not greasy yet, but it has tools.
Her ruler has Mickey Mouse.
Together they build a basket-weave fence around the yard.
He wears his dark blue coveralls, but this time his cap says
"Allwoods" and teaches her to saw and nail.

Standing at the lathe with my brother, he teaches him to cut threads.
Again, in blue coveralls, but this time his cap says "Lobo Engines."
He tips his cap shielding his eyes from the light.
Taking the micrometer from his box, he tells my brother, "You
must always be accurate—at least to a thousandth of an inch."

When he buys tools, he buys three.
One for my sister, one for my brother and one for himself.

I try to learn about tools but the hammer is too big for my hand
and I bend the nails.
The saw gets stuck in the wood as I cut.
I want him to be my father too!

As I prepare to leave home I pack my toolbox.
It's a small, cardboard box.
Light, unlike my father's.
Inside are flat wrenches, hammers and pliers cut out of paper.
I have no micrometers or rulers.

I've made my toolbox and my tools, since my father only buys three.

Cecile Turrietta

Homenaje A Papá

(Murió 10 agosto 1975)

Murió como vivió
A todo dar.
Nunca creí todo aquello que me dijiste.
Unicamente, que yo era de tu sangre, mi viejo.
Ecuentro en los mil y un recuerdos
Laberintos, que casi sin querer, te quise.

Te recuerdo como fuiste esa última primavera
Usabas anteojos para leer y dirigir y
Rastrabas un poco la pierna izquierda.
Rebozabas de ideas y conclusiones,
Ilustrando cada palabra con arabescos arte a mano.
Ebrio de la vida, feliz como siempre y como nunca.
Tamaño de un arbusto, y grueso como tamal
A la vez duro como árbol, y picante, y natural.

Pues ya te vas, y no nos dijistes ni
Adiós ni nada.
Pensamos que tu vida sería para siempre.
Ahora sabemos mejor, pero ¿cómo se explica?

(My father only used one "T" in his surname.)

Petimetra

La felicidad también a mí me toca.
Así sucede que me conviene más
Amar que ser amada.
Mejor andar sola por el mundo
que mal acompañada.
No nací para pasar la santa vida
Aguantando ni los deseos ni las pesadillas ajenas
O para disimular ni agradarle a un fulano de tal
Que me imponga litanías de faenas.
Andale pues, mi buen señor,
Cóntestame de mero macho
¿Tú también no prefieres amar
Sin estar rigorosamente AMARado?

Nuestros Vecinos

Las Comadres
Photograph—Linda Montoya

Marian Baca Ackerman

Vecino Vicente

Señor Mares awoke with a startled cry as he hastened out of bed and shook Señora Mares, "Mamá, se murió Vicente." Señora Mares requested that her husband return to bed as he probably had had another bad dream. Señor Mares insisted that this dream was a message from the departing soul of his life long friend and neighbor Vicente Martínez as the ninety year old man had been gravely ill and expected to die any time. With this Señora Mares arose and proceeded downstairs to the kitchen to prepare coffee. After a cup of the strong black beverage, Señor Mares filled a jar with the remaining coffee and left slamming the door behind him. He walked briskly through the stretch of field directly behind his home to the horizontal adobe house where Vicente had lived alone since the death of his wife fifteen years ago. As was custom, he entered through the small back door and with quickened steps, advanced to the sala and into the north bedroom through an arched opening in the three foot adobe wall that enclosed the bedroom with the pink quilted bedspread. Flinging the curtain open in haste, he perceived the pale breathing face of his good vecino under the flickering velita that Vicente always kept lit beneath the nicho where he kept his beloved bulto of Nuestra Señora de los Dolores, the one he himself had carved. No, he was not gone yet, gracias a Dios, but from Señor Mares observation he was very close to death. Kneeling beside him, Señor Mares asked Vicente if he would like some hot coffee. Vicente's large dark eyes were luminous in contrast to the ashen color of the ascetic face and taut white lips. "Oh, Vecino you have come in time to help me prepare to meet my master. You received my message." Vicente then told Señor Mares to notify the brotherhood to prepare him as they had his earthly father. Señor Mares

111

made no mention of calling the priest because the customs of the Penitentes as he knew them were different. Vicente requested the presence of El Hermano Mayor and the many friends of his brotherhood.

Señor Mares knew that Vicente had spent the early years of his boyhood in Taos, New Mexico as an orphan in a seminary school. The only child of an unwed mother, Vicente was five years old when his mother died of weakness and consumption. Alone, without grandparents or close relatives, Vicente was taken in by the kindly well-known priest of the area who ran a seminary for young local boys in Taos and the surrounding countryside. Vicente had often told Señor Mares that he was not the only orphan who was given refuge, an education, and the name of the priest. On his deathbed, Vicente recounted briefly from flashes of memory about El Padre and life at the seminary as he had actually been one of his last sons. El Padre was well in his sixties and suffering from ill health when Vicente was a tall and lanky teenager. Vicente often served at mass during Padre Martinez' last years in the small chapel that was erected in his home.

Being the only father Vicente had known, he maintained a great love for him the rest of his life. As a youth, Vicente said, he was continously encouraged by El Padre to continue his education and carry on his work by going into the teaching field. After El Padre's death, Vicente attended the Normal University in Las Vegas and his life's commitment had been that of a school teacher in rural New Mexico. Señor Mares had often heard Vicente reiterate, "The good that he did could fill a book. He took me in and many like me and we were given food, a home and an education to the best of his ability. Perhaps not to match El Obispo's nor the French clergy's for we had neither the universities not the libraries of the great cities of France. We were not exposed to the art, architecture, music and literature of civilized Europe. We did learn to read and write and think. Even perhaps to think more freely like the early fathers of the desert, for we resided figuratively in a desert. In this desert we were close to nature and to God. We were not distracted by the finery of the civilized world. In this desert, we led good lives. We expressed and executed bultos, santos, retablos that came from the depths of our soul. In this desert, our faith was not encumbered by trappings."

Vicente's adobe home was cramped by noon. Los Hermanos de la Fraternidad de Nuestro Padre Jesús Nazareno were singing their alabados. El

Hermano Mayor was close by, giving his blessing and praying with Vicente. When the body was expiring, el Resador empezó a gritarle a Jesús. Executing the ritual y la encomendación de alma, he shouted the name of Jesús three times commending his soul into the hands of the father. Two brothers extended their hands gently over the body's middle section and a third gently held the head to give a comforting assistance to the expulsion of the soul and spiritual body, making upward movements from his feet to his head. They placed a wooden slab with dirt at his feet and rested his feet upon it. They then gave him water continuously, as water was the one thing the spiritual body could make use of while trying to free itself. Then followed the preparation for the Velorio. The brothers washed and dressed the body of Vicente and wrapped it in a mortaja, enshrouded it in a white sheet and, with its bare feet, placed it on a table surrounded by velitas. Many candles provided warmth at the feet thus facilitating the spiritual body's final expulsion through the head and the severance of the silver cord.

Friends and relatives brought food for the supper that evening and bonfires were lit outside the home. As the men gathered to visit around the fires, the women remained indoors, preparing la cena. Though people entered and left the parlor constantly, the body was never left alone. Alabados were sung throughout the night and the rosary was recited at midnight. A final alabado was sung at dawn. Since the priest was out serving the missions, the funeral was taken over by the brothers the following day and Vicente was buried in the cemetery. When the priest returned there was a Requiem Mass and a blessing of Vicente's grave the following week with the brothers, friends and relatives present.

Señor Mares reminisced during the blessing of the grave and recalled Vicente's desire to be prepared for death as his earthly father had been. There was only a minor difference, thought Señor Mares. Though a sprinkling of Vicente's hermanos attended the funeral, there were large groups of Los Hermanos de Nuestro Padre Jesús from every morada in New Mexico at El Padre's funeral, numbering two thousand, Vicente had told him. Señor Mares could almost see Vicente and El Padre rejoicing in their heavenly morada.

With uplifted head, Señor Mares quizzed the air. Since El Padre was a defrocked priest, was there a Requiem Mass for him? Then with a speculated reply to himself, he whispered, "Yes, of course there was, Los Hermanos would have seen to that."

Denise Chávez

The King and Queen of Comezón

Excerpt from a novel, *"Beatriz"*

It is summer and Arnuflo Olivárez stands between the sun, shielding time. Arnuflo is unofficial Good Will Ambassador and Master of Ceremonies for the Fiesta in the small town where I grew up, the world I continue to haunt.

Arnuflo is surrounded by his daughters, the half and the whole: Lucinda, who is Fiesta Queen, and Juliana, who sits in her wheelchair, her twisted flesh in her metal throne, a scapular wound twice between her hair bows of pink and white.

Arnuflo stands bejeweled, in his silver and gold sombrero from Juárez, fusing sunlight into diamond tears of day.

Juliana sits up front, in the center of the plaza kiosco, in her place of honor, next to her sister, the Queen, with the smile of a contented seraphim.

"I'm jest fine," Juliana coos, "I'm jest fine, it's so good to see you again. How you been?"

And how have *you* been, Juliana?

She answers with a look of no small wonder.

"At the house, descansando, resting, you know..."

Twisted Juliana with uneven breasts, and what does it matter if they are there at all? Saint Juliana blessing her father, and he, yelling out, in the booming voice of growing older men, "Buenas noches, damas y caballeros, caballeros y damas, buenas!"

Olivárez, the enchanter, struts a hello. "Buenas noches, bienvenidos a la Fiesta."

Arnuflo is dignified, with a pumped-up walrus face, His tiny blue eyes are the eyes of a shrewd boy, a dauntless lover. His overlapping grey mustache, once black, dangles across fleshy lips that sputter and spray. With a hand too enormous to hold, to be held, he twists and twines those impudent hairs, those oozing words. A large belly and truncated torso support a turquoise studded bolo tie and matching concha belt—a gift from the City Council, on behalf of the citizens, their gratitude.

Arnuflo wears a grey charro suit with glass insets that nestle like glowing fish eyes in the light. He is the color of the sun that shines in the eyes of older young men and young old men, eyes transmuted and transformed into golden glass that bounces off the charro suit, that royal attire, that befits a king, the King of Comezón.

Arnuflo is animal like, unrestrained, his trembling eyes bead and break with joy. They are unquiet pilgrims, they wander about the plaza, seeking out faces, impressions, momentarily resting on his padded Tony Lama boots. His feet are the feet of a large robust man, splayed outward, without consideration. He is awesome, all of him, and the voice that bellows greetings is the voice of the untamed father, the wild brother, the fatal lover. He speaks earnestly, "We are proud of Comezón." His speech is a prayer, "We are her brothers, we are her citizens, we are her men, and yes, her women, and she gives us life, health, mercy. We are here to celebrate the annual Fiesta; we are here to give thanks to God, who has given us this time together."

Arnuflo stands in the center of the plaza's kiosco, hands upraised, exhorting the locals to pay heed, rejoice it is May 1st, the one of many May 1sts that are now but vapors of sentiments, photographs of children, running, smiling, crying. Those children who now laugh, threaten, display and taunt.

Arnuflo Olivárez stands, revolving prism of the town's light life. He is color, form, assurance. He is an old man crystallized in time, standing in the growing dark, beseeching all to dance...for the night is getting cold. We wrap our arms in shawls, pull into coats and draw ourselves inside—the time of nights is not quite here. Give us a while, soon the Río Grande will flow proud, high, impregnating the land—her banks laden with the seeds of future passions. Lovers will sprawl there, their flesh cooled by the nights unchanging willingness to hold. And on talking to a friend from Texas, this is what we settled on: that there were no words for these nights, for they exist on the crest of dream, and that we, having witnessed them, *know* them, the length and breadth of summer, herself, the moist madness of her, her charms, her dripping, hot impenetrably lush hopes. So—as one anticipated the darkness of room, the lovers hands, one waited, for Arnuflo, for the fiesta, for the dance that signalled the beginning, for us then, the initiation into nights, those nights which drew us, hungrily into the swirling crowds where faces circled round, but only eyes were real.

In groups of two or three, the girls sauntered past their mothers' booths, those booths where posole, frijoles, tacos and hamburgers were sold — driving smells of chile and hot lard into the air, permeating the nasal passages with the lingering odor of aunts' houses, feasts days, weddings, and days of mourning, when the family of the bereaved would not cook, were not allowed to cook, but accepted food, and were fed royally by relatives, friends, comadres, all of those who had known the deceased when there was breath, a chance, food, song.

The girls walk slowly, lingeringly, careening past young couples who float by, lost in their miraculous union. The girls, plump, little-eyes, with hard firm breasts or else, lost girls, in white halter tops, in jeans or shorts, with valleys of untouched flesh, half-confused looks encounter boys, crazy boys, with cow-licks, and tee-shirts, boys in faded jeans, farm boys, who live with their abuelitas, boys who huddle in groups, smoking, laughing, sighing. They are the night's boys, the boys of growing older women, half-grown, wondering, lusting boys. Boys. Boys. And the girls—with painted eyes, are made-up for them. They all circle round—the boys—the girls—moths—not dancing, but clinging to the light—to the dream of future encounters, to the hope of the flesh, the fevers, the flowing nights. They cling.

Arnuflo introduces Queen Lucinda. Daughter of. Student of. Future graduate of. Future wife of. Future Mother of. Lover of this night with its colored lights. Lucinda stands, her train carried by others. Little girls trace her shadow, she is enshrined in turquoise, a crown befitting the land—a sunburst of molten sun, surrounded by the blue of moon. Her fingers drip metallic blue, she dances now with Arnuflo, her father, who holds her, tiny leaf to his leaden chest. He binds her to his frame, she frets steps away, unable, and having to—is released, and thankfully returns to her handmaidens, children between the ages of three and five, pages, minions of some higher order and sense of beauty. They stare at her with their painted eyes and

Queen. She sits, to reign. The circling boys her other, dearer pages, the lonely, lovely girls with their untouched flesh, her true handmaidens.

The mothers of these girls are soaked in grease, and sweat, the smell of meat and pod, the fathers are drenched in beer, peddling loops, racing tired mice, hustling rides, the Merry-go-round, the small metal cars, the horses. The Mothers, the Fathers, they are upholders of the myth.

And it was here, when I was a circling boy, that a friend of my parents approached me. Mrs. Benavídez, a small yelping woman who kept belching. Her ringed, red lips and eyes of tense fidelity drew me to her, "Josefía, Josefía, such a pretty boy, such a pretty boy, let me hold you." In her whimpering, watering eyes I could see lost shadows, feel some vague sadness. "Come here, come here, aren't you going to give me a kiss?"

Arnuflo's voice raffled time. A side of beef was won, a guest was introduced, Dr. González from the University, Mr López from the Governor's Office, he couldn't make it tonight, I'll read the telegram...

Who listened? Who knew? Unsettling hungers paced between trees, we clenched our cold flesh. No...it wasn't time—not yet. It was May 1st, and the summer, her moistness, her moodiness, was just intimation. It had snowed up North this May. This was New Mexico. Who would deny the constant imbalance between desert and shade?

Arnuflo fretted. Did Lucinda need a drink? Where was Mrs. Olivárez? Was Juliana sleepy and want to go home with Isa, face like a metate? It's your bedtime, querida.

Juliana was flushed. She had sat, primly, knees bound by invisible wires, hands folded over onto themselves, surrounded by flowers, yellow chrysanthemums, all afternoon and night. She had sat, smiling, attentive, humming to herself, little girls' songs, while the children hovered about her, tending her, fanning her with their devotion.

It was Juliana, not Lucinda who was really Queen. Juliana sat, her malformed torso propped up on the metal arm of her throne, crowing and laughing with delight and unconcern. She was in no hurry. Arnuflo's house lay at the edge of the plaza, and what awaited her, but rooms? Here in the plaza she was the sky, and more.

It is now that I confess to you my love for her. It was Juliana that drew me, May 1st, a young, confused boy, so many years ago, into the hope of night.

She, with her tafetta little girl's dress, she, a woman of thirty, her lips red as women's darkest blood.

Her smile, her laugh displaced all the other wandering girls. And when she was wheeled away, to her room, that room of impenetrable depth, that room, she called her own, with a white tufted bedspread where I imagined she lay and had no dreams, but slept as all innocent children do, without any recollection; I turned away, folded myself into the night.

Spirit mother, I had lost her to the Moon, and where was my Beatrice? Gone.

Gloria G. Gonzales

The Woman Who Makes Belly Buttons

She put a fresh white apron on, straightened her short hair with her finger tips and pinched her cheeks for more color. Since she is the first person a baby sees, she likes to look her best to greet her or him.

Her name is Jesusita Aragón, known as Tita to her many friends. Five feet tall, stocky, she wears her reddish-brown greying hair short and tightly permed. Her rosy cheeks, thick glasses and butcher-type apron have become her trademark. At 79, she is one of the oldest practicing midwives left in our generation. She has been delivering babies for 65 years and claims well over 12,000 babies born into her hands.

When I first heard of her in Las Vegas, New Mexico, her name was synonomous with baby. All my hippie friends were delivering with her. We thought it was a continuation of our anti-establishment movement. Upon meeting her I learned she was a legend in her own time. She not only delivered hippies' babies, but those of native, anglo, student, straight, hip, old and young women. On my first visit I met a teenage mother-to-be who herself had been delivered by Jesusita, escorted by her mother into Jesusita's trusted hands.

A native New Mexican, I had been delivered at home by my grandmother who was a midwife. But in 1973 my own mother's attitude had changed. She wanted me to go to a hospital. My husband, Chip, being from New York, thought all babies were born in hospitals. His opposition ended after his first meeting with Jesusita. Although she spoke little English and he no Spanish, I interpreted and they shared the universal language, a smile. When we left, Chip said, "Yes, I trust her with you and our baby."

Although we lived 25 miles out of town, we were nested at a friend's house in town, next door to the hospital. We could hear the doctors being paged to the emergency room or to the delivery room, so we knew we were safe if there were any complications in delivery. Jesusita had explained why she couldn't come to my home to deliver my baby. She pointed out how disappointed I would feel if I came to town in labor to discover that she was in Mora or another neighboring town assisting another woman. By only delivering in town she would assist up to three women simultaneously.

She joined us at 5 a.m. after several checks in the night. She assured us we would deliver by dawn. We were going to name a daughter "Dawn." But labor continued. Her peace emanated so deeply that the pain was relieved. "This baby will be born when its time comes," she'd offer encouragingly. Dawn came and passed, as did the sunrise, as did morning. Our relationship was so intimate during this long labor that she asked if I would like to study under her as a midwife. I did not know the answer.

At the point that I might have screamed and accepted drugs for relief, I knew that we were in transition and the time had come. At 11:17 a.m. the head emerged. She had a friend pour a bottle of olive oil to aid in easing it and the shoulders out. A girl. Her feet and hands were the color of a New Mexico sunset on the purple shade. As Jesusita rubbed the umbilical cord, the shades changed to a sunrise pink, thus her name, Zia Pilar. (Strong Sun). She then had my husband rub my belly for delivery of the afterbirth. While I held this naked bambina, clean from her olive oil bath, Jesusita gracefully tied the cord explaining that it was a priceless gift being wrapped, that this navel would one day show when wearing a bikini.

Forgetting the intensity of labor, I finally answered her question. "Jesusita, I think my gift is having babies, not catching them." She laughed. For this wonderful service, prenatal care, counseling, guidance and inspiration, her fee was fifty dollars.

On occasion I would stop to visit Jesusita and there would be a birth in process. She would invite me to stay. Because of continued pressures from the State for her retirement, she liked having personal support with her. When I, a stranger, entered the room these families always welcomed me.

In Jesusita's suitcase, along with her tools, a pan for the placenta, sterile string for the cord, scissors, a rubber suction bulb, a portable scale, medicine for the babies' eyes, and Vaseline, she carries pictures of my children's births.

The most difficult birth I witnessed, even more so than my fourteen-hour labor, was the evening I dropped by and the impending father asked me to stay and take pictures. When I entered the room, Jesusita said in Spanish, "Es muy difícil." As nobody else in the room spoke Spanish, I smiled, wanting to reassure them. I questioned silently why I should be at this place at this time and accepted it as something meant to be. As I stood at the foot of the bed, the mother, about to deliver her second child, was in the late stages of labor. Jesusita whispered again softly, "Está atravesado." (It's breech). The mother looked at me and although my mind flew in a thousand directions— fear...run...why me?—I continued to smile, ignoring Jesusita. When the mother, feeling secure, turned away, I responded, "Entiendo." I decided since I was there I would use the greatest power I know, Prayer. When what should have been the head crowning but was actually a tiny buttock emerging, the mother's friend standing to my right said, "The head is coming." I wondered if she knew and was trying to assure her, but as her husband joined in the excitement and encouraged her to push, I knew I was the only other one who knew the truth or saw Jesusita holding and pulling tightly as though against the law of gravity. The mother screamed, "This is too hard, it's not the same, the second is supposed to be easier," but the movement had to progress quickly. My prayers were oral now and everyone seeing the situation cheered, "Push, don't stop." And, with great expertise, Jesusita pulled this baby out. It's tiny feet were hooked over its shoulders. The mother was relieved, joyful, and understanding of the difference in delivery. This was confirmation of Jesusita's philosophy given to her by her grandmother. You never tell the woman if the baby is breech, because fear will make her contract rather than push, thus risking the baby's life. Jesusita testified in support of a doctor being sued for his license after the death of a breech baby he assisted. She explained to the judge that if the mother is aware or afraid, her own muscles can lead to the death of the baby. The doctor was acquitted. During a natural birth, after the head has emerged, there is a pause during which the shoulders are turned. In a breech, there can be no pause.

If there wasn't a birth happening I'd spend hours listening to her gold-spun stories. Jesusita was raised outside, like a boy, herding sheep and goats, harvesting, hauling water. When her grandmother went to deliver, riding side-saddle, Jesusita prided herself in being able to wear jeans and ride straddled alongside her. There were no circumstances that prevented the midwives from reaching their patients. "One time a man came to bring me to his wife. He arrived riding a beautiful stallion and brought a gentle but swayback mare. I walked out and told him, "I will not go anywhere on that 'garapata'. My father, knowing my stubbornness, laughed trying to explain to this neighbor that I was a capable rider. I mounted the stallion and left the gentleman arguing with my father that I would be thrown. I shouted to him that I would have his baby delivered before he returned on the mare."

Jesusita had much experience in watching the animals she cared for deliver their offspring and she had the experience of learning from her grandmother who had learned from her mother. She delivered her first baby at the age of 14. Her grandmother went out to deliver a baby some 40 miles away. Jesusita's nearby aunt was not due for another week. While Jesusita tended the sheep, her sister called for her help and she assisted in her aunt's delivery. Her grandmother was so proud when she returned that from that point Jesusita began her lifetime career. Although she only had an eighth grade education, she learned from the best and continued taking required courses for nurse-midwives in the area.

"My mother caught one of the epidemics of those days. After her eighth baby girl, who only lived about an hour, was born, my mother died. I was only 7, but became like a mother to my 5 and 3 year-old sisters. We lived with aunts, uncles and grandparents."

"My first troubles came when I was 23 and got pregnant. My boyfriend says he doesn't care and the rest of my family gets mad at me. In those days one followed the *dieta* after having a baby. Which meant at least 8 days in bed, 15 days indoors and 40 before one could do any hard work. The woman remained on a special diet and was not allowed to fully immerse her body in water nor wash her hair. She was allowed only to take sponge baths. Anyone who did not conform to this rule would indeed suffer during her change of life. My family made me work during my pregnancy, banned me from dances, and even from going to church because I had shamed the family name. Although my grandmother helped me deliver an 11-pound baby boy, Ernesto, I was still treated poorly by my family. I was forced to go out in the fields and work, without the respect of the *dieta*." Jesusita says the emotional depression and responsibility for a baby as a single mother have given her much compassion as a midwife. When women cry in pain during labor she knows the pain intimately. I remember screaming during one contraction, "Jesusita, help me!" She said, "I can't help you." After another contraction I screamed, "God help me!" and she giggled, "He can help you."

It wasn't as though she had not had enough bad luck, being rejected by her family, but when she became pregnant again, they treated her as though she were invisible. She delivered her 10 1/2-pound baby girl, Dolores, alone.

Though her father had remarried and had another family, Jesusita's loyalities were to her sisters. Her youngest sister also became pregnant and was thrown out of her father's house. Jesusita helped Ramona build a house next door to hers there in Trujillo, but for the six years after the birth of her son, Ben, her sister's health continued to fail. Jesusita raised her nephew after Ramona's death at age 29, but mourned deeply the friendship she had lost.

Although she was an outcast, her loving nature was always there for her father or grandmother when they needed her. She would work in the fields with her father even though he had not spoken to her for three years after the birth of her son. She took her grandmother in to live with her after the death of her grandfather even though she had been rejected for so many years.

Jesusita moved into town, Las Vegas, when Ernesto was in high school. She wanted him to have the opportunity for the good education she was denied. She supported her family by cleaning houses, doing laundry, and delivering babies. Eventually she worked at the parachute factory for 11 years. It was after work that she found time to build her own home where she lives today with several additions that she had built throughout the years.

She had to leave work several times to deliver babies and eventually was confronted by her boss. After showing him her license, he allowed her the free time to deliver babies. He also allowed pregnant women to work until due date, saying Jesusita was there if they needed her. He also lightened their work loads and wouldn't let them lift heavy loads. Jesusita repaid him by working late hours and agreed to every contract he assigned her. She loved to sew and was the only experienced person to "darn." Darning socks, a skill her grandmother taught her, now made her a specialist. They brought parachutes from other places for her to darn.

"Besides babies, and work, my greatest love is dancing. Even though they made me quit going when I was young, after we moved to Las Vegas, we would go to Trujillo on Friday nights. Soledad, my younger sister, made me go to a local dance one night with her. I won my first dance contest that night. Ernesto, who lives next door, comes over and dances with me and sometimes I go out with him and Dolores and my grandchildren. The next day everybody says their feet hurt, but I feel wonderful."

It was between pregnancies that I went to see her after being treated by doctors for kidney, bladder infections, or a tubal pregnancy. In spite of all the medication, I was still in pain. She checked me, said it was a tilted uterus, lifted it and, in seconds, after one month of pain, it was gone. She prescribed herb teas and exercise. I've never suffered from it again and have taken many other women to Jesusita with the same symptoms, all experiencing the same immediate relief.

My first child was eight months when Jesusita confirmed that I was again pregnant. Each labor progressed much quicker. The second was only two hours of hard labor. Chip claims I had my first son so quickly just to beat him at cards, saying he had the best spade hand in history at the moment Joaquín wanted out. I especially enjoyed this pregnancy as a dear friend of mine, Marg, was also pregnant. We spent Thanksgiving and Christmas together with our husbands making plans to have our babies on the same day and time at Jesusita's. I can remember the January day we drove into town, the snow storm behind us, and the disappointment we felt when we pulled into Jesusita's house and our friends' chevy "Big Red," was not in the driveway. When we entered, Jesusita announced that Bart and Marg had left for home with a baby boy an hour before and she was presently assisting another woman. Her cheeks were so rosy and she looked radiant in her excitement over triple births in one day. After my examination, she confirmed we were on our way to delivery. As she had encouraged me, the second was easier.

It was rumored around this time that Jesusita was losing her vision. Another "she must retire" reaction. I was to have two more children with her, knowing that her hands were sighted enough. The rumors have not yet been able to drown her reputation. Her vision today is excellent.

Our third child Giovanna, is the only one we had at Jesusita's house. We arrived from Albuquerque at midnight. I was not in labor. She set a bed for Chip who would have to go to work by 6 a.m. My friend JoAnne and I stayed in the "Maternity" room talking the night away as we had not seen each other in months. Jesusita awakened and came in at 5:45 and said, "We may as well examine you again." I was in full labor, ready to deliver. When we woke Chip he was truly surprised to enter and find us in the final stages of labor. Giovanna was born at 6:20 a.m. Besides the hospital bed and its comfort (a new addition since my first delivery), what I enjoyed most was the focal point in front of the bed: a large three-foot painting of Christ with angels surrounding him at Passover.

Jesusita does much more than stand by and attend each birth or merely catch or turn a baby. She dedicates her hands to God, thanking Him for the gift he has given her and her very presence seems to draw one's pain. She was a strength I needed. I laugh about this birth because although the fee was still only fifty dollars, being five days after Christmas, we paid for this child in installment payments.

My fourth child was born under extreme circumstances. On my due date I stopped by to visit Jesusita who was attending another woman. She explained to me that this was a long and difficult labor and asked me to encourage the woman to walk around. It was a gorgeous Indian summer day. I suggested that she and her husband go window shopping or for a walk around the plaza, one of my favorite pre-labor pastimes. She yelled at me saying I didn't understand her pain. This was her first baby and I stood about to drop my fourth. She refused to leave the bed. In the next room Jesusita examined me and said I would be late as there were no signs of labor yet. After I left, Jesusita called a supporting doctor who came to her house and urged this young mother to go to the hospital. Although Jesusita uses no medical instruments she instinctively knew about fetal distress. The woman got dressed then refused to go. Her baby was stillborn.

There was a black cloud over the community as many blamed Jesusita for negligence. It was 10 days later that my husband and I sat in a restaurant at about 6:30 p.m. I was eating lightly as I had that gut feeling that "today was the day" though I hadn't had any labor pains. We had placed our other children, ages 5, 3 1/2 and 22 months with neighbors. Sitting in the cafe, I flinched and my husband knew the time had come even though I had merely invited him to a movie. We picked up his brother, Michael, who was to be our photographer and drove to our friend, JoAnne's. We listened to her play the

piano and visited, expecting the evening to grow long. At around 8:30 I got
out of a warm bath as Chip returned with Jesusita. She examined me and I
suggested we sit in the living room to listen to JoAnne play. She said, "I pre-
fer that you stay lying down." Within a few minutes she put on her apron and
I knew she had missed her cue. My body didn't feel anywhere near delivery.
Several contractions and 20 minutes later, Santino was born. The first person we called was the local doctor and the black cloud was lifted. She thanked me for the confidence I had in her. The birth pictures show the cord
slightly wrapped around my son's neck, separated by two of Jesusita's
fingers. She asserts she always inserts two fingers at the neck once the head
emerges for this reason alone. She says it is not uncommon as the cord has to
go somewhere. Where depends on its length. She protectively does this in
every delivery.

Retiring as baby maker, I continue to find reasons to make frequent
pilgrimages to visit Jesusita and after all these years, there are still many
stories to hear.

"Not so many women have babies at home. Not so many women have
babies. I think it is because of birth control. I think birth control is a good
thing. If they had it when I was young, I wouldn't have gotten in trouble and
maybe my life would be different. Still my children and grandchildren are my
life and I wouldn't want to change that."

In order to support herself during this slow season, she began taking in
boarders from the State Hospital nearby. She houses them in what used to be
her main maternity room. Her busy house consists of two bedrooms for
boarders, her bedroom with a double bed, two sitting chairs, a wooden
kitchen chair, a dresser, the top filled with pictures of relatives and friends
and statues of saints. If she has several guests at the same time the bed serves
as a couch. If a neighbor is visiting and a client enters, the neighbor quietly
exits, as they have respected her profession for a long time. The next room is
now her main delivery room. There is the hospital bed, the wooden chair
with arm rests where Jesusita sits waiting through labor, a table with her suitcase filled with needed tools, and a chest of drawers, filled with books and
ledgers of all her patients and deliveries. To get an accurate number of births,
she claims would take months of study of the ledgers and we could easily
wallpaper her house with certificates of birth she has on file. "Don't forget

26 sets of twins and 2 sets of triplets," she adds.

Her kitchen is well organized. She cooks there for her boarders and family and will offer a meal to the attending family.

"Once I asked a doctor why children don't obey their parents like they used to" and he said, "these children are being raised on animals' milk and are more aggressive than those raised at their mother's breasts."

Jesusita has witnessed droughts and death, feasts and festivals. She has lost babies at birth and has come to know that these things happen. "That's life. It's not easy, but life goes on." Her grandmother taught her, "see what you see, but suffer it quietly." Her advice to future midwives in regard to abnormalities is that they come with the trade. Her grandmother predicted she would in her life see babies born walking and talking. She says I will see it in my lifetime. Babies used to be born weak and lazy. They lay still for six months. Now, they hold their heads up at birth and look around the room. They smile immediately. She has had some grab at her apron with a tight grip. One phenomenon she witnessed: she and the family were sitting in the kitchen while the laboring mother-to-be rested. They heard the baby cry and Jesusita ran into the room believing the baby had come on its own. But the baby was still within the womb though the five of them heard its cry.

On May 15th the Governor honored Jesusita with a "Jesusita Aragón Day" and a benefit dance held in her honor in Las Vegas that night. Present were many of her "babies from 2 months to 64 years old." We watched her dance the night away. On Sunday, July 12th, she was awarded the "Living Treasure" award in Santa Fe and, on October 23rd, she was honored as Midwife of the Year nationally at a M.A.N.A. (Midwife Alliance National Association) convention in Denver.

In spite of these tributes, Jesusita is saddened. She took the State licensing exam and failed by only 10 points. The State Health Department has failed to issue her the Granny license she claims she was once promised. A licensed midwife has agreed to tutor her in preparation for the next State exam. She is not ready to retire. She says she is still in good health and believes she would know deep within when her time comes to quit. She recalls a few years ago when she broke her leg and had to refuse women who wanted her to assist them. "I knew my limitations and would again know them. I want to retire when I feel the time is right not when someone tells me I have to."

Jesusita had a six-month stretch of appealing to the Governor for a Granny license and having to refuse patients. "I may not know how to use a stethoscope or fetal monitor but I know these things instinctively. I shouldn't be punished for that." Her status now is unclear. But she delivered her first baby after this break and, since then, her appointment book is filling up. In fact, she missed the ceremony in Denver because she had two babies due during that weekend. This baby, who broke the fear barrier, is my Godchild. She was the first of what may be the last. Knowing Jesusita was there with all her experience and skill was worth the risk of not obeying someone else's edict saying where and how a woman can deliver her baby. I witnessed this birth and Jesusita's magic still exists. Her retirement will have to come to her from God because it doesn't appear as if anyone else has succeded at stopping her.

When this time comes, I envision Jesusita becoming a teacher to a new generation of midwives. For whether it is this year or next, leaving behind a tradition, a legend of love, will be difficult for all of us who have known her, for those who today want to know her, but hardest on Jesusita, who knows one thing: she knows how to deliver babies and how to make belly buttons.

Reynalda Ortiz y Pino de Dinkel

Peregrinación a la Tierra del Luminoso

Los peregrinos huicholes, que emprenden el camino del peyote, caminan con brazos cruzados sobre el pecho. Las caras todas grabadas del silencio están alumbradas de espiritualidad. De la grandeza inmóvil del desierto, los matorrales, los nopales, y los huicholes han sido esculpidos. Se siente un recogimiento en los hombres, que marchan por entre las cactáceas esparcidas, camino a la tierra del Luminoso.

Y yo, como uno de esos muvieris de plumas de águila que guardan en su petaca cuando no están en uso, sin oficio camino con ellos. Avanzo por la polvorienta semivereda con los huicholes porque Tani, el Maracame Tatevarí, representante del fuego, me ha traído con él. Soy padre Franciscano. Ha trabajado a mi lado este Tani viejo y correoso que quiere convencerme de que esta peregrinación huichol es tan llena de religiosidad y de rito como cualquier ceremonia de las mías.

Tani, que va explicándome las cosas, es buen trabajador en la misión. Me hace sonreir porque visto de soslayo, así como lo veo ahora, parece que sus estaca-piernas sostienen su panza con dificultad. Es panzudito. Y es una mezcla rara de religión. A veces es *él* el sacerdote como lo es hoy.

Los huicholes son grandes peregrinos, y Tani es el peregrino de los peregrinos. Mi padre San Francisco hubiera amado a este Tani que viaja con dignidad aquí a mi lado.

Lo que nosotros vemos como una piedra o como una planta, para ellos es un kakaullari, un ser que resistió las pruebas de la creación y al nacer el sol se quedó transformado en roca o en arbusto. Algo de esto trata de explicarme Tani que encabeza la marcha de sus feligreses que levantan el polvo a cada paso.

Cuando mi amigo, Maracame Tateverí, representante del Fuego, decide descansar descansamos. Cuando él dicta, "Aquí haremos la fogata para la purificación," allí se hace la fogata. Nadie habla. Estamos llegando a un lugar poblado de dioses. Alguien le pone la silla ceremonial, el uwene, y Tani se sienta. Ya no es Tani. Es el sacerdote de los sacerdotes. Bajo el sombrero, que días antes decoró con plumas de guajolote y colas de ardilla, sentado en el uwene, con el bastón de su oficio en una mano, y el muvieris en la otra, es Maracame Tateverí y requiere atención y respeto. Ya antes de sentarse había puesto los bules con el tabaco sagrado a su ladito, como si estuviera poco dispuesto a separarse de ellos. ¿Y por qué no? Los bules, después de todo, con el tabaco sagrado de poder mágico nos han apartado a los animales y a los diablos del camino.

—Traigan aquí sus huaraches, les dice. Yo voy a limpiarlos para que los conduzcan sanos y salvos, para que ellos los guien y los aparten de los alacranes, de las serpientes y de los diablos del camino; para que los lleven aprisa y descansadamente a la Tierra del Luminoso. Así lo hicieron nuestros antepasados y así lo haré.

Uno trás otro los huicholes se acercan con los huaraches en la mano. El Macarame Tateverí, que antes era mi amigo Tani, limpia los huaraches con el muvieris. El muvieris está hecho de una vara cubierta de hilo que sostiene amarradas algunas plumas de águila. Todo buen chaman tiene siete o cinco muvieris. Fuera impotente sin la ayuda de ellos. Gracias a estos muvieris de místico poder se puede cantar y curar, conocer los disignios de los dioses, saber todo lo que pasa en la tierra, en el cielo y destruir las maniobras de los hechiceros.

—Hemos llegado al Cerro de la Estrella, al sagrado lugar donde vamos a confesar nuestros pecados y donde quedaremos limpios. Todos debemos confesarlos. El que oculte uno solo será castigado por los dioses.

Todos los huicholes se retiran allá lejitos. Queda solo el Macareme Tateverí que antes era mi amigo Tani, y ahora es confesor o lo será cuando se acerque el primer valiente. Ahora permanece atento, cargado de bules y muvieris. Su gran sombrero emplumado le cubre la cara. Se acerca el primer pecador que con la cabeza inclinada, sin mirarlo, le dice en voz baja sus pecados. A cada pecado, Tatevarí hace un nudo en la cuerda kaunari que cada penitente le ha de presentar para llevar registro de los pecados.

La soberbia, la avaricia, la gula, la ira, la envidia, la pereza no son transgresiones capitales. Así es que nadie confiesa que ha sido soberbio ni avariento ni goloso, ni colérico, ni envidioso, ni siquiera perezoso. Sus pecados se reducen a uno solo: la carne en sus menores implicaciones. Había cuerdas con quince o veinte nudos. No registraban unicamente los hechos consumados, sino una gama de intenciones: roces accidentales, deseos, miradas, encuentros fortuitos.

Terminada la confesión de los peyoteros, frente a la hoguera, hacen una nueva confesión general. Luego entregan las cuerdas a las llamas. Casi ni chispearon las cuerdas cargadas de nudos del único pecado, la carne. El humo subía de la fogata. Los ojos vidriosos de los huicholes, que ya quedan descadenados del pecado, siguen clavados en la hoguera. La limpieza ritual me los ha preparado para comulgar con el Divino Luminoso. Ya no incurrirán en la cólera del Dios Peyote. Ya podremos seguir la peregrinación.

Tani, que ya ha oído los pecados de los peregrinos, y que ha anudado cuerdas tiene un no sé qué de sobrio. Será porque hemos llegado a la región donde todo es sagrado.

Bruscamente hace alto Tani. A sus pies se halla un charco. Tani-Maracame-Tativerí-confesor-gobernador se despoja cuidadosamente de los objetos del culto: muvieris de plumas, flechas, jícaras, botellas con sangre y de agua traída del lago de Chapala. Descargan sus cestos todos los peregrinos. Entonces coge Tani una flor, la moja en el agua y les da de beber a cada uno de los peregrinos. Los veo sorber el agua sagrada.

Salimos en fila otra vez. Cruzamos una pequeña lóma y no tardamos en pisar el sagrado suelo de Viricota. ¡Pero si esta peregrinación ha sido toda una fiesta ritual! ¿Qué va a hacer ahora Tani-sacerdote? Sin dar señas de fatiga humedece unas hojas secas de maíz. Vierte tabaco en las hojas. Hace después los bultos y se los entrega a los peyoteros.

—Aquí les doy el tabaco sagrado, el Corazón del Guego. El sabrá guiarlos hasta donde se encuentra escondido nuestro Hermano Mayor.

Parecen ser palabras sacrosantas estas palabras, porque se iluminan las caras de los feligreses de Tani, que ya poco le queda de Tani y mucho de sacerdote.

Pero esta ceremonia no basta. Todavía tienen que someterse los peregrinos a otras antes de poder salir en busca del peyote. Tatevarí Maracame ha encontrado el primer peyote. En finas rebanadas se las da en la boca a los peyoteros. Sin abrir los ojos mastican el peyote lentamente. Hacen ofrendas a los dioses.

Al fin concluyen las ceremonias y los peyoteros se dispersan en busca del peyote. Es un duro trabajo. El peyote-Hermano Mayor-dios luminoso está oculto bajo la maleza. Es difícil de localizar. De todas las cactáceas es la menos espectacular. Es una humilde y pequeña cactácea. Pero por fea que sea debe su fama a sus ácidos perturbadores.

Cubiertos con sus sombreros emplumados, deteniendo en la boca el bulto del tabaco sagrado, los peregrinos continúan cortando peyotes y echándolos en los cestos. Cortan peyotes y piensan en la prueba que los aguarda al caer la noche. Esperan los dones de los dioses.

Regresan al campamento espinados y llenos de arañazos. Parecen soldados que regresan de alguna derrota, así todos cansados, sudorosos, y decaídos. Se ponen a descortezar su rica cosecha de peyotes. Los parten y sus pedazos los atan formano collares. Después sentados alrededor de la hoguera, comen sus peyotes y comienzan a hundirse en el éxtasis. ¿Qué oyen y que ven? En el trance Tani ya no es Tani; ahora es místico que espera comulgar y hablar con los dioses. Espera algo concreto de la divinidad oculta en el cacto sagrado.

Ya en otra ocasión mi amigo Tani me ha contado algo de sus experiencias mezcalinianas. Cuando está bajo los efectos del peyote oye los cánticos de los dioses, de los árboles de las rocas. Oye sus palabras misteriosas y resonantes. Ve salir del fuego a Tamatz el dios-Venado. Lo llega a ver transformarse en extrañas y luminosas flores. Las flores se convierten en venados azules, y los venados azules en nubes, y las nubes en lluvia que cae sobre sus milpas.

Aquí tengo de nuevo a Tani que ha descorrido los velos que ocultan el porvenir. Camino a casa, ya sin las vestiduras de su sacro oficio, cargando su cesto lleno de peyote, parece Tani-huichol; parece huichol como los demás de los peregrinos. Ha tenido su ascenso místico. Ha comulgado con un dios.

Laura Gutiérrez Spencer

El Romance de Danny

¿A dónde vas mi niño?
¿Qué hicieron hijo?

¿A dónde vas mi amor?
¿Y qué he hecho yo?

Desde el día en que viniste
A tomarme el corazón
Al castillo arrogante
Asaltaste al torrejón

Hambriento de la frente
Caballero juguetón
Conquistaste el demente
Dominaste la razón

Triunfante y glorioso
Tu bandera ascendió
Furioso el emblema
Y valiente el color

Satisfecho en conquista
Tu espada se rindió
Embriagado de la hazaña
Bajaste noble, puro y señor

Y ayer te vi en el parque
Como siempre te hablé
Manso contestaste
Sombra sólo te hallé

Y oigo por el aire
Que huíste de la ley
Y preso te entregaste
Sin orgullo y sin fe

¿A dónde vas cariño?
¿Qué te hicieron hijo?

¿A dónde vas mi amor?
¿Y qué te he hecho yo?

Desde el día en que viniste....

133

Cecile Turrietta

Cosas Que Pasan

Como les iba diciendo...aquí en Barelas
    Nobody told us we lived in a barrio
    that everyone didn't speak Spanglish
    and you could not take burritos for lunch
    but you found it out at school.
There were things we "just knew"
    pachucos tattoed blue crosses between their thumb and index finger
    and used lanolin to comb their hair into a duck's ass style.
    de llamativo, girls drew black beauty spots with eye-brow pencil
    on the cheek bone or just below the lip.
And you knew when you were "en casa" because
    the dueño said, "Entre, sígale, sígale, ésta es su casa,"
    adults said to children "mijita" this and "mijito" that
    you're supposed to say "usted" to everyone big
    and the man who delivered coal was not ese cabrón.
And you always wondered how much longer until
    you could eat posole and tamales on Christmas Eve
    make the altar for the fiestas of la Señora de Guadalupe
    sing "Mañanitas" for someone's birthday
    the mariachis started to play rancheras at the church bazaar.
And there was a time
    when all the girl babies had pierced ears
    and abuelitas always wore black and a scarf on their head
    everyone wore a scapular or a medal and owned more than one
    rosary,
    and if the chile was really hot, it was OK to quemosiar.

And you always expected
   the sun to shine, and meat to dry on perchas for winter jerky
   chile made into ristras to be hung outside the kitchen door
   adobe houses to be dark and cool inside
   and to add water to the pompa and jump back when water gushed
   out.
And all your friends and their friends
   dressed in Sunday clothes to walk in the Corpus Christi processions,
   cried at velorios as they said "lo siento mucho" to dolientes
   had padrinos and compadres and primos...more than one could count
   prayed to Tata Dios and paid to light candles in the church.
Unas palabras se podían usar, otras no
   la plebe never quite understood what
   a la vequia...úchala...bolillo
   really meant but you best be careful where you used them
   and if you called someone
   pendejo...lambe...mitotero
   you better be bigger than them
   but just to be part of a conversation, you could say
   a la máquina...hijo la...chanza...órale ese.
And when you were somewhat older, more maduro, you learned that
   making tortillas come out round is an art in itself
   that the policía and políticos are always suspect
   when speaking Spanish you had to use your hands
   you wanted to be known as gente de buen barro.
Válgame Dios, por tanto se me olvidó todo esto.

Nuestros Paisajes

Untitled
Lithoserigraph—Delilah

138

Cordelia Chávez Candelaria

Echoes Of A Flat Earth

It's true the planet's round.
Spherical as a wet tennis ball
Not plastic perfect as a cultured pearl
Not bulging here, bruised there, and moist
With the blood, fears, and occasional sweat
of its teeming players.
Earth's true shape and motion stagger thought.
How do the mountains hold on tight?
The oceans wave without spilling dry as broken glass?
Awesome thought—even a tiny baby
Sunning gently on a helpless summer lawn,
Filling the air with its tendersweet joy
Is held close by that love hug, gravity,
Not spun off into some galaxy's black hole.
We have come so far—we know it's so.
We know that nebulae and even quarks are so.

So when I heard the dearest of dear people
Was banished from her children, banished
From her children because because beblah
Blah blah born lesbian her orbit swung another curve.
Suddenly
I felt how razor flat this world is
And sought to walk right off its brittle edge.

Delfina Rede Chávez

El Río Grande

En serpentina línea,
por montañas, por bosques,
por cascadas y por llanos
sigue su curso interrumpido,
sereno, tranquilo, audaz
y hasta ladrón

Sus aguas límpidas, bondadosas
han dado de beber al sediento,
al pastor, al conquistador,
al labrador y al caminante.

Aguas tan limpias como
el cristal que retratan el cielo
y la gloria de Dios.
A veces pueden ser lodozas
color de muzgo y de pecado
y también
han sido traidoras, asesinas
y vengadoras.
Por siglos como un imán siguen atrayendo
al deportista, al turista,
al pescador y al moderno explorador.

Tú que divides países, culturas
y naciones, sigue tu misión.
Continúa sembrando paz,
alegría, y serenidad y alimentando
a miles.

Eres como las culturas
que albergas, una mezcla
hermosa, conglomeración de razas,
que se tornan en una sola,
al contemplar por tus riberas,
el cielo de más hermoso azul
las noches del más verde verdor
días de brillante sol acariciador.

Sé el buen amigo al niño
lleno de admiración y expectación.
Da fé al adolescente que lleno de sueños
y fantasías, también alberga pensamientos
lúgubres y dudosos.

Al anciano de mirada tranquila
y triste que muere viviendo
el recuerdo de su juventud.

Te conozco desde niña
en el suave murmullo acariciador,
y también te conozco en
el esplendor de tu poder y majestad
embravecido, enorme,
terrible, y aterrador,
arrastrando a tu paso
sembradías, humildes chozas,
animales y nidos humanos.

Tú Río Grande, tranquilo
y sin remordimientos, con audacia
y sagacidad cambias tu curso
y robas terrenos y los conviertes
en chamizal
Juegas, y te diviertes con tu poder
de rey y Señor.

Aunque sediento de poder,
desde tu virginal nacimento
en las montañas del Colorado,
hasta el Golfo de México,
has sido testigo por siglos
de sueños, de aventuras, fracasos,
de gozos y de risas.

Por esto se te ama, por tu vaivén acariciador,
tu ruido y cascabeleo y tu tranquilidad serena.

Por eso se te necesita, porque eres eterno,
porque eres fiel.

Sigue pues, tu carrera interrumpida,
tu implacable poder se torna
al viejo Río Grande, dulce, apacible y acogedor,
por eso, Río Grande, se te ama,
y se te perdona.

Juanita M. Sánchez

Return

barrio atrisco
actually, we never thought
of it as a "barrio"
it was only atrisco

dirt roads
adobe church
houses
and a thousand dogs

trips to the outhouse
in six inches of snow
you learn to hold it

i took to the skies
landed in san antonio
texas
thinking the air force
would change things

it did
atrisco is different
the roads are paved
but they left the holes in

the dogs
they die now
on the 'paved' roads

some things never change
the church
my father

Linda Sandoval

La Luna Es Una Mujer

The dark sky lights up with her untamed brilliance;
clouds dance around her, they relish her presence.
Esto sí lo sé: La luna es una mujer.

Anxiously awaiting her moonbeam caresses,
twinkling stars compete for her undivided attention.
Esto sí lo sé: La luna es una mujer.

Full, quarter, half—
the skyline is enchanted with her curvature persistent.
Esto sí lo sé: La luna es una mujer.

Gently, dusk arrives but this lady doesn't mind
she knows the heavens are her forever playground.
Esto ya lo sé: La luna es una mujer.

Las Mujeres Hablan

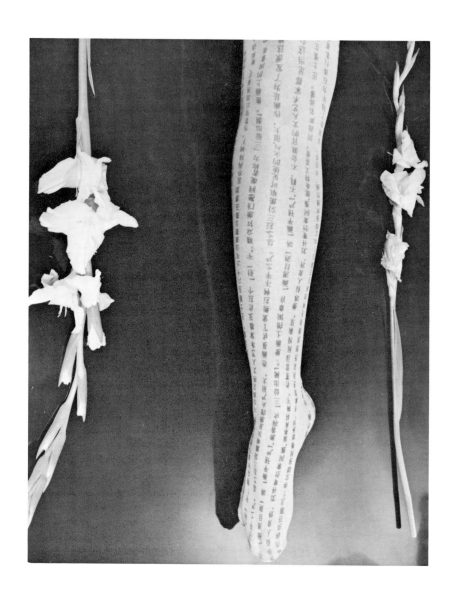

Other Women Series
Handpainted Photograph—Soledad Marjon

146

Elena Avila

Free From The Past

It's the weird way I say good-bye
to you.

I burned all love notes. Gave away
your gifts. Some of them I threw
away in rage. I used sage to purify
the "letting go" ceremony and sealed
it with a ritual.

No trace.....I want no trace of you.
You who betrayed me.

Sometimes, out of nowhere, I find
another reminder of you; a bookmark,
a poem you wrote. I have to decide
all over again if I really do mean
"no Trace".

Today, I found a notebook you used to
carry around with you. I remembered
that you wrote me two poems on the cheap
"Red Chief" pad you thought was so cute.

As I read them again I realize I haven't
thought of you for a long, long time.
The poems are written with love and care.

I'll keep them, I decide. I'll keep the
notebook too.

Coming Home

Mama! Mama! I've been so cold without
you...
The big city does not hold me like you
do Mama....

It doesn't have your roots as you hold
me tightly to you...the wind as you
whisper your lullaby.

Your fine desert sand as your womb...
like the ocean so long
ago.

Oh Mama...your sweet smells as I nuzzle
close to you! My senses so like
excited children..
taking you in...your wild flowers, sage

rain and damp earth–I could lie in your
arms forever.

Oh Mama! I've been so cold without you...
the big city does not hold me like you
do.

Fall, 1983

In The East

I said good-by to him in the West. The place of
  reflection and ultimate death.

I grieved for him in the South...my howls so much
  like the coyote in the loneliness of the desert
                                            night.

I gathered power and wisdom from the North. Mis
abuelos, Virgen de Guadalupe, and Malinche urged
  me on with their ancient dance.

I let him go in the East....the place of new
  beginnings......the place of new births.

I no longer need his reflection. I let him go in
                    the East.....

Cordelia Chávez Candelaria

Poem With Explanation.

I.   This part is a story poem.
                Thursdays were her days for traveling.
                On Wednesdays she took the empty suitcase
                out of the closet and filled it with cotton
                metaphors.

II.   This is the history section.
                Her family used to move around a lot.
                1st grade was five schools
                learned A through F in Deming, G–L in Alamagordo,
                M–R Roswell. Missed U through Z–people
                passing through parenthetically.

III.   This part's an experiment in style.
                            d r i f t
                            r i f t
                              i f
                                i
                      ay ay ay ay

IV.   The explanation follows
                : : : :

♀bject

What's the point of knowing
a Virgen Mary miracle hallowed Spain in century one, A.D.?
Another one in Mexico
made it easier to tranquilize the Aztecs in 1531?
What's the use of knowing
Joan of Arc saved the French at Orléans?
She was burned to ash at last like a wornout wooden doll.
History's women appear before us in matchless purity and pain
        and so—
we try to match them
how they looked and acted
we try to climb their pedestals
like kids shimmying up trees.
But habits—booming, bombing, balling—
slip up traction and we slide back down the pole.

So I object to role models
that end up rolling over me. I object
to all pornography—
mother, sister, daughter, aunt and me
as cheesecake icons of kink or cleric,
I object to porn, whatever form.
I am *subject not*

            "Objection Overruled"   *(second voice)*

Note: Legend has it that the cradle of the Spanish Catholic
Church goes back to the miracle of *la Virgen del Pilar* occur-
ring in the first century to St. James the Elder. A similar miracle
occurred in Mexico in 1531 with the appearance of *la Virgen de
Guadalupe* to an Indian peasant, Juan Diego. Blessed with
divine power, St Joan is credited with the French victory at
Orleans in 1429.

Evening News

———————————child playing   supper cooking———————
near naked strangers
                break in
                        strike the peace
                of this simple air
                        ATTACK
it's the real thing
mugging for money
                between minutes of Nicaragua
                                or jobless workers
                with a better idea
                for early Mondays than queuing
                on gaunt hopes
                this time luck will
                reach out and touch a joy
like the pink flesh pressing new & improved love
in toothpaste poses
gleaming strangers smiling
                between minutes of Port au Prince poverty
                where children play tag or Ma Tante
                to forget suppertime's come and   gone
                skipped away like a hopscotch   trinket
                tossed too hard
                please don't squeeze the   hard truth
(quote:)
                "the United States last year
                spent 90 BILLION DOLLARS on advertising"
                                        (unquote)
————————MURDER   on the evening news———————

Delfina Rede Chávez

El Crujido

El crujido de mis huesos
lo ignoro por completo
Porque aun
Sé soñar
Sé añorar
Sé amar

Lo ignoro por completo
porque ya en lontananza percibo
la luz
la esperanza
De un mundo
desconocido
anhelado
soñado

El crujido de mis huesos
viejos, cansados,
se ignora
se olvida
Ya que es el pase ineludible
a esa luz imán
Que se percibe ya en la distancia
Que casi se busca
Que casi se anhela
Que ya casi se espera

El Baño

La anciana, decrépita, solitaria
y triste,
prepara su baño.

Cuidadosamente recoge lo necesario
para su limpieza,
Ya que su belleza se le ha escapado.

Esas manos que un día
fueron orgullo de sus mejores años
Ahora trémulas y frágiles
toman el jabón perfumado
y la esponja importada.

Casi con reverencia, suavemente levanta
y lava doblés tras doblés
de su arrugada piel
que asemeja a un viejo acordeón
un acordeón que un día tocó.

Que no fuera concierto mozartino
sino música "bien"
Música romántica, llena de amor
y de sueños, e ilusiones
que se mutilaron al nacer.

Baño, bálsamo sanador,
energético sin par
tu alientas y mitigas
y yo te bendigo.

En el baño, se medita, se proyecta,
y se recuerda,
la niñez
la mocedad
la juventud

Como en una pantalla se desliza lentamente
la vida
que se re-vive
que huye
que se escapa

Y esto, la anciana ¿lo acepta,
o la rechaza?

Denise Chávez

Love Poem

I remember Mikey grinding his pencil into my back
the smell of Sister Alma Sophie's false teeth
the taste of pomegranates from the convent garden
wide, round, juicy red

My prayer for all women:
fruit and the silence of large
open high-ceilinged rooms
where other women can hold them
and not expect anything in return

I am grateful to Lydia
who never having met me
greeted me with an embrace
joined me at the waist and breast

Both of us rooted to the floor
we felt a bolt of lightning
pass up from the ground
into and through us
and bursting into flame
she held me, dying

And Amber, healer,
who took over when the Doctor could do nothing
for the headaches
the shoulders
the burdens
the grief

Up the stairs to her room
we went that first time
let me hold you
but how?
I was there to be counseled
not touched

For an hour she held me
in that small bed in a room slanted
my twisted back to her
pouring out dreams
ghosts pummeling me
mercilessly

Thank you, Sister Alma Sophie
for your faith in me
for your irreverance
you juggled the votes in 8th Grade
and voted me Most Talented
I knew you rigged the whole thing
it was I who counted the votes

I remember your hard face
and sneaking looks between the black veil
the white band
trying to see what color your hair was
if it was short
and how the heavy cloth molded your breasts
the place where breasts should be

I speculated on your sexuality
and thanked you for the pomegranates
brought from your garden
the lush dark secret place
near the old Safeway
now both torn down
the corner of Las Cruces and Alameda
that is where you nuns lived
Sisters of Divine Providence

I visited you there
with Christmas food
cookies and bread
gifts from other women without men

The pomegranates you reserved for few:
Mikey and me
he was travieso, naughty, Sister,
ground his pencil into my back
twisting it into my flesh
I was afraid to tell you
that he was hurting me
so I remained silent
ate my pomegranate seeds
one by one

My prayer for all women:
shaded gardens
burning pomegranates
light filled beds
with spirit sisters

Margo Chávez

Je Reviens

Rosalinda thought she could speak French. She knew the name of a
French perfume, and even what it meant. "Je reviens:" "I'll return." She
liked to use it on those occasions when she would return. I taught her how to
say, "Je regarde:" "I'm looking," to use in all those perfume shops we
entered, to hold off the imperious French shopgirls. They knew too easily
and too well how to demolish one's self-confidence, and reduce one to a non-
entity, those French shopgirls, with their pointed nails, their pointed shoes,
and their pointed hearts.

Rosalinda walked in the street practicing her phrase: je regarde, je regarde. A few people turned their heads. She walked into the shop repeating
her phrase under her breath. The shopkeeper laughed, an enjoyed laugh.
Rosalinda would ask, in a mixture of English, Spanish and perfume French,
to try out a certain perfume. Rosalinda had short arms and a great number of
perfumes to try, so we sometimes entered two or more shops a day. We could
do that if there was some perfume along the length of her arm that she didn't
really care for, or if the scent had sufficiently disappeared, or if there was left
a virgin patch somewhere on her short soft arms. The shopkeeper gathered
the different demonstration bottles, or we followed her humbly around the
store to the Guerlain section, to Rochas, to Christian Dior, to Chanel, to
Jean Patou. The bottles and their boxes sat elegantly on glass shelves,
enticements to luxury, lures to passion, to romance and dark, secret moments. I loved the look of the bottles more than I cared for their scents. There
was something infinitely womanly about the smooth glass bottles or the
multi-faceted glass bottles, each a signature of femininity. I coveted a long
low dressing table with linen and lace to cover it, on which to set rows, double

rows or triple rows, of a universe of womanly glass bottles of different shapes and different colors, with atomizer pumps on the end of a purple or black cord tassel, or with long pointed stoppers which you lift off delicately and brazenly, to dab behind your ears and in other dark secret places to match those moments. I desired a dressing table with objects of womanhood displayed there, as they were in my mother's long white dresser: round glass boxes that hold loose, scented powder, brush and comb sets that lay expensively on a matching tray and don't really brush your hair very well, and here and there a stray black hairpin, escaped from my mother's dark, long hair. The peinetas that she used lay there too. Of course there are the rows of perfume bottles. My identity displayed on a dressing table.

My dressing table does not look like that at all. There is not one bottle of perfume on it. There is no lace and linen cover. There are two lacquer boxes, one on each end, with drawers that hold my magic secrets of jewels and paints. There is a low round box, not of glass, not holding flesh-pink scented powder, but a flowered Russian box, a gift from María, where I put my barrettes. My mother didn't wear barrettes; I don't wear powder. There is a Gauguin postcard stuck in the mirror with a poem in Spanish from a lover. There is a dry yellow petal fallen from a rose, poignant tribute to another, old lover. It will stay there until someday I brush it away. Two books are set there.

Is this the right dressing table? Have I properly displayed myself? Where are the bottles of perfume that hold my identity, trapped like a genie, released when the cruel stopper is pulled out, to dab behind the ear in that timeless feminine gesture?...the scent slowly evaporates.

And the scent evaporates from Rosalinda's arm. So we walk into another shop. More bottles, different passions. Expanded possibilities.

Today Rosalinda has run out of arm. She sprays the chosen potion inside the front of her blouse. Usually we walk down the street sniffing our own and each other's arms. I see that Rosalinda today pulls out the front of her blouse and smells there. The man walking by turns to look, I giggle, but as they do, I imagine dark, secret moments, moments to whisper, "Je reviens."

tesamaechávez

Secrets

I could close my eyes
to open the knife
and slice out a piece of cake
too burnt on life nobody wants to eat.

I could close my eyes up tight
and coil myself just right
'til the blackness inside
turns white.

Lorena García

Fallen Women

We are not the fallen women
We are the women
that have not yet risen

        para que nos entendamos bien
        a nosotros nos empujaron, tiraron para
        abajo,
        aplastaron por arriba

No, we are not the fallen women
We are the ones that got up and went.

Luto

      Que ingenuas somos las mujeres.
      Antes creíamos que nuestras
      madres, abuelas y hermanas
      se vestían de luto
      porque se les había muerto
      el marido/martirio
      pero, no,
      el luto se lo ponían
      cuando descubrían que eran
      Mujeres.

Porfavor

Porfavor
No me llame señorita
Yo soy LORENA
Lorena—a secas.
Vengo por un sólo mes
y la verdad es que
No me merezco el título de
Señorita.
No,
YO SOY hija de la sra.
hermana de la señorita
sobrina de tal
prima de fulanita
amiga de sutana y mengana.
A mí, como a ti
nos gusta la fruta
    cuando
       c
       u
       e
       l
       g
       a
  del arbol   l^{e}
              o s^{a}
                        de la tierra
así, natural.
Si, tú también eres tierra
de Temuco,
    mapuchita.
También le prohibo
hacerme la cama
y ordenar mi pieza.
No se preocupe No
le gritaré: tráeme
las manzanas peladas
y con azúcar.
A mí no me gusta
quitarle ni agregarle
nada a la fruta.

El Apio Rojo

Yo vi un apio,
no era un apio verde.
Un apio rojo, rojo
como el clavel.
Ahí en el basurero
del baño
sangraban ramas rojas.
Del cuarto de María
salía llanto, llanto.
Ahogada en la almohada
lloraba
"La sra. me echa si sabe,
mi niña, se buena."

Ese día yo tiré la basura.

Inside/Outside Still Inside

We are told to stay inside,
at home
and remain virgins.
This is what we must do
to become the right kind of woman
(the kind men want and look for).
But to become a man
he must go out and take a woman
although that sometimes means
entering a whorehouse,
where women still remain inside.

Darwin says Women are Genetic Mute-ta-tions

When I was small
I had a dream that often repeated itself:

A crone takes me by the hand
and makes me open a closet door,
hundreds of tongues fall on me.
Tongues and more tongues
swim and roll
around my ankles,
reaching up to my waist,
licking me and seeking touch.
Some are old, dry and cracked.
Others flap wet with saliva,
like fish out of water.
The crone helps me up
pushing and slapping them down,
these tongues hiss at her, and steam.
The crone then leads me to another door.
Obediently, I open it
and from it hundreds of women run
reaching and raking at the tongues
with their nails,
trying to find their own,
a tongue
with which to speak to men.

Huacha, No More

You yell out to me
"Ahi te watcho, huacha."
You think I am alone, abandoned
like some mis-placed shoe.
You'd like to be right
but you're wrong.

I carry protection.
I travel with hundreds
of women inside me
they are all here:
Eva, Medusa, Magdalena,
Safo, Quiltrala y las demás.

I have a right to walk
on the streets, you know
without, being her-assed/harassed
My sisters and I won't let you.
Our scream will be forever
ringing in your ears.

From now on you need to remember:
women travel in packs of one.

       *huacha—by oneself, orphan

Scrambled Eggs/Huevos Revueltos

I have a friend.
She thinks she's a good egg.
My friend has a husband.
He's an egg beater.

I feel like an egg, she tells me
sometimes soft,
sometimes hard boiled
but most of the time, fried,

I'd like to beat his huevos, I tell her.

He gives her everything
diamonds, fur coats
carros nuevos, todito
including black eyes.

After a session of real communication
he cries and se arriepiente.
He promises her el cielo y la tierra.
She swallows his words, sus lágrimas.

They love it/each other.

He showers,
washes away his sperm
his anger
leaving his pride clean.

Her marks don't wash away
they remain like the broken egg shell
waiting for the day
for him to finish the job.

The Same Difference

We have the same child,
yet we speak to him differently,
in different languages.
You tell him of the things he will do as a man
hunt, fish and kill.
I tell him of the things in the world he belongs to
I give him other weapons other than spears and guns
I give him language.
You exclude him
while I include him.
Let's not tug at his arms too hard.

Marcella Lucinda García

Rosa Blanca, Rosa Negra, Rosa...Colorear
White Rose, Black Rose, Rose...Grow Red

It was the house of the Lord she had entered.
She had come in despair, consumed with guilt,
knowing she didn't belong here.
She fell to her knees, still the words would
not come.
She felt a presence and turned to see if someone
was near.
Doña Luz glared at her; her sparkling blue eyes
revealed hope.
She rested her hands on Anna's shoulders and
spoke,
"God forgives my child, God forgives."
And she was gone.
The words flowed freely from Anna's trembling lips,
"Forgive me Father, for I have sinned..."

     *   *   *   *   *   *   *   *   *   *   *

.....The chants and screams echoed as they welcomed her to hell. The
mangled fetus lay floating in a pool of blood. In the midst of rising flames, a
burning hell prepared to devour another of its children into the breath of its
powers. The slithering black serpents gliding, forcing their way amidst the
screeching orange scorpions and swallowing spiders who feasted on human

flesh. Anna held on to the thread-like cord. The pit below her forced echoes; useless cries of those who had come before her. She could feel the heated flames and hear the screams of sinners who had met their destinies. She had been warned that hell would be like this. The prayers to la Virgen were of no use now. The thread-like umbilical cord which she grasped for life disintegrated in the flames; splitting in half, denying her, as she had denied it. The flames scorched her flesh and the heat seeped into the depth of her soul. Her spirit sank into the flames, screaming in unison with the chants and the cries.....

"No!" Anna screamed as she awoke and grabbed the rosary beads from the headboard behind her. "Ave María Purisima!" she prayed, as she took the rosary beads, running them through her sweaty fingers. Her light brown skin glistened, warmed by the perspiration that dampened it. She stared into the mirror which hung on the wall at the foot of her bed; staring into eyes that stared into hers; eyes instilled with fear, pleading for comfort, a hope that the pain revealed within them would vanish. As she shifted her eyes to the rosary she recalled the nightmare, its vivid images returning to her memory. In desperation she flung the rosary to the wall. "What good is this?" she cried as she watched the beads scatter and roll about the floor.

She could remember why it all began...Juan. The bar. Too many margaritas. The drive home. The deserted road. Juan's insistence. "No!" she had begged. Her torn dress. His rough hands. The pain. The blood. The abortion.

.....A girl of seven, long curly black hair, innocent rootbeer eyes, and soft brown skin kneeled at the altar to accept the Eucharist. It was her first time. The first confession. The months of studying the Catechism had paid off. Mamá and Papá would be proud now. They watched as little Anna, in her white holy communion gown repeated the words of Father Martin. "I accept the body of Christ," the soft voice spoke. Mamá and Papá turning towards one another, smiling, as little Anna recited her prayers to la Virgen. Pride filled their eyes as they listened to Anna perfectly recite the prayers of the catechism.....

The vows had been made many years ago. She could remember the very prayers she had repeated that day. Turning back to the mirror, Anna stared at eyes, eyes that beckoned for answers. "What am I to do now?" they asked, "what am I to do now?"

"Que Dios te bendiga, my child," Doña Luz said as Anna made her way out of Doña Luz's home. Anna hadn't expected to spend the entire afternoon visiting with the viejita she had met at the park, but Doña Luz had befriended her at a time when she did not need to be alone...

The cool Spring morning air brought with it the signs of the new earth. The hummingbirds sat on the old oak trees, flocking together and scattering about to make room for the others. The green grass was spreading its soft blanket over the shades of yellow, transforming it into its rebirth. The birds' chirpings softly harmonized with the peacefulness, signifying the rebirth of the new Spring and its replenishment of life.

Anna walked in circles, ignoring the birds nestling together on the old oak trees. The cool morning air brought goose bumps to her skin. The sun seemed to follow her as the rays formed on her silky black hair, yet she seemed oblivious to her surroundings. She didn't seem to notice the hummingbirds, nor the blanketing green grass, nor the blossoming of the yellow daffodils that sprouted out of the new earth illuminating the awakening of Spring. She paused to blindly stare at the little children grasping tightly their mother's hands, as their smudgy round faces gleamed and they pointed up towards the sky and spoke in soft harmonic voices, "Lookee Mamma, see the birdies."

She didn't look up to follow the pointing finger of a small boy who paused to admire the birds. She continued to walk. The birds continued to sing. The flowers continued to blossom. The children continued to enjoy.

"Muchachita, ven acá," Doña Luz called as Anna walked past her. Anna stopped, turning her head to glance at the frail viejita who had called to her. She continued to walk until the words of the viejita caused her to pause. "Sin vergüenza," Doña Luz yelled, "y no tienes respeto para tus mayores?"

Anna turned and walked towards la viejita. Standing in front of her, Anna stared into la viejita's face. She smiled at the memory the viejita evoked. Mamá came to her mind; her constant commands echoed in Anna's memory, "obey and respect your elders." She glanced into Doña Luz's eyes. Her thoughts suddenly shifting as an overpowering sensation seemed to be pulling her towards la viejita. A force seeped into her pores, taking complete control over her. Anna walked closer towards the old woman as she was rising from the bench, struggling to grasp her cane.

"Yo soy Anna"

Doña Luz stared into Anna's eyes. "Algún día," she said, "algún día vas a saber."

Anna turned away, her face changing colors as embarrassment seized her composure. She bent down to pick up Doña Luz's shopping bag and handed it to her.

"Me llamo Luz," she replied, taking the bag from Anna's trembling hand.

"Mucho gusto conocerte," Anna said as she forced a smile. She again focused on Doña Luz's mesmerizing eyes, awed by the ocean blue reflections they revealed. Stories of hope, innocence, struggle, and survival gave Anna a glimpse of the life Doña Luz had lived. The several wrinkles displayed the wisdom, while her smile revealed the youthfulness embedded within it. The smile brought comfort to Anna; a comfort she believed she would never feel again. Suddenly, Anna turned away, realizing what she was doing. She turned again to face Doña Luz as if apologizing. Doña Luz returned the stare, piercing into eyes that presented images of fear. She quickly stepped away; her smile disappearing as she read Anna's eyes with an expression of disbelief. Anna turned away. Doña Luz slowly walked towards her. "Ven," she said, taking Anna's hand and leading her out of the park.

Anna walked with Doña Luz as they entered the neighborhood barrio. She felt a strange warmth and secure feeling as she looked around at the boarded windows on the old, peeling stucco houses. The older abandoned houses were covered with graffiti; spray painted with black words like Los Vatos, Mariella con Miguel Por Siempre, and Los Locos Rule. Old beat up cars filled the driveways and backyards. The smell of roasting chile verde permeated through the air. Cholos and cholas hung around the street corner, dressed in khaki attire, black muscle shirts with la Virgen Guadalupe embroidered on the front, and red bandanas wrapped around slicked back, black hair. Little children playing canicas near the road; their high pitched voices echoing to remind Anna of home.

"Buenos días le de Diós, Doña Luz," squeaked a small boy with a red kool-aid mustache donning his upper lip.

"Buenos días Santiago," replied Doña Luz, smiling at the boy and patting his head, "¿cómo estás?"

"Muy bien señora, gracias," he replied, fingering the small cat-eyed marble and piercing into the crystal shades of its colors. He glanced up occasionally to look at Anna.

"Adiós, Santiago," Doña Luz said, as she pulled Anna to continue on their walk.

They arrived at the project housing and turned the corner to Number 6 to enter Doña Luz's front yard. Doña Luz fumbled in her shopping bag and retrieved the key.

As Anna entered she could smell the aroma of fresh tortillas on the stove, probably the tortillas Doña Luz had prepared for the morning breakfast. She smelled the distinctive aroma of old age; the same smell mixed in with the burning firewood of her abuelita's stove back in El Valle. She entered the small living room and observed the knicknacks that sat on the shelves of Doña Luz's barren living room. Anna walked towards one of the shelves to view the pictures in the oak wooden frames while Doña Luz walked into a bedroom and sat her shopping bag on the bed, placing her shawl on the coatrack and closing the door behind her. Anna took one of the wooden frames, expecting to see the smiling faces of Doña Luz's children and grandchildren, but as she looked at the picture, she found it odd that it was not the type of picture a mother would display with pride. Instead, it was a picture of Vienna. Anna sat it back on the shelf and looked at the others and saw that they, too, were photographs of foreign places: Rome, Paris, Greece and Buenos Aires. She took another frame and stared at the young lady with blond hair and ocean blue eyes dressed in a habit and posing with Pope Paul. It was then that Anna realized that Doña Luz had been a nun and that the photographs were of the places she had been to on her journey to serve God.

Anna looked around at the small living room of Doña Luz's home. Who is this old lady, she thought, and why am I here? She looked again at the pictures of Doña Luz with the Pope and felt a strangeness. "How could I meet up with a nun, when I, myself, am doubting my faith?" she asked. Nervously, she turned towards the closed door to the bedroom Doña Luz had entered. Anna wanted to turn and run as images of her life at the Parish School came to her memory. Sister Florencia, her seventh grade teacher, focused in her thoughts. The anger Anna knew that Sister Florencia would show because of her inability to understand, brought goose bumps to Anna's skin. She walked towards the front door when she saw no sign of the viejita she had met at the park. Reaching for the doorknob, she paused. She could not leave. She had not followed Doña Luz willingly. A force beyond her control had brought her here. Anna turned around and waited for Doña Luz to return.

Doña Luz walked out of the bedroom into the kitchen, poured some café and gestured for Anna to join her. She placed a plate of biscochitos on the table.

Anna walked into the kitchen, pulled a chair from the table, and sat down. Her eyes gazed at Doña Luz, as Doña Luz was struggling to pull a chair and sit on it. Doña Luz reached across the table and taking Anna's hand in her own, asked "¿Qué pasa con mi hija?"

"Nada," Anna replied, as images of Sister Florencia once again returned to her memory. Her eyes winced as she re-experienced the pain of the ruler slapping her hand for giggling with Sophia, her best friend at the Parish School.

"Tell me," Doña Luz insisted, "tell me. I will help."

Anna hesitated. I have no other hope, she thought, maybe she will understand and help me. "I am afraid," she began, "I am afraid of what I have become." Doña Luz held Anna's hand tightly as she watched the mirroring fear instilled in Anna's eyes. "I was raised a Catholic and I promised to follow the vows and live by the ways of the church, and I don't think I can believe anymore. I have broken the vows and I am gradually losing my faith, and I am nothing without my faith."

Doña Luz looked around the kitchen. I see the church has failed you too, she thought, give your life to it and it throws you out when it can no longer support you. "What have you done, my child?"

"I had an abortion," Anna replied, staring into Doña Luz's eyes and anticipating the slap she know would soon follow.

Doña Luz turned away.

"I was raped!" she screamed, "I had to do it!"

Doña Luz turned back to face Anna. The blank expression on her face caused Anna to bow her head down in shame. "I cannot judge you," she said, "I cannot condemn you, although I have been taught to. Anna look at me," she said, stretching her hand and lifting Anna's chin, forcing her to look at her. "I understand," she said, "I understand why you feel as though you cannot hold on to your faith, when you are given no reason to." You have been taught wrong, she thought, we have both been decieved.

A sparkle filled Anna's eyes as tiny tears illuminated her mirroring brown eyes. She had expected Doña Luz to turn her away, condemn her also, like Sister Florencia had. The images of Sister Florencia, slapping her across the face and dragging her to the Mother Superior to suffer the wrath of her sin, rapidly flowed in her thoughts.

Doña Luz rose from her chair and slowly walked towards Anna. She embraced her, taking her in her arms and holding her until Anna calmed down.

"God, He won't forgive me. He won't forgive me."

"God forgives, my child. God forgives."

Doña Luz stared into Anna's eyes. She could see in their reflection that she, too, had somehow taken part in filling eyes of innocence with fear. "Anna, listen to me," she said, "you must listen to me if I am to help you. I can help you find forgiveness from God, but first I must help you to find forgiveness within yourself." Doña Luz paused. The silence lengthened into an eternity as Doña Luz remembered her life in the convent. This will take more than just prayer, more than just penance; this will take much more than that, she thought.

"Doña Luz, are you okay?"

"Sí, estoy bien."

"Can you help me?"

"Sí," Doña Luz replied, her mind made up. "First of all, I must tell you that I know how you feel and I understand what you have been made to feel. Faith is a terrible thing to lose. It is I who brought you here. I knew nothing of what it was that caused the fear you walk in. I sensed your anguish at the park when you walked past me. I felt your weakness, your despair, yet I also heard your plea. I called to you to help you, but you feel as if you are beyond being helped and you would not come. So, I brought you here anyway."

"How?"

"My child, I was blessed with a gift. It is much too difficult to explain, but I promise to explain it to you soon. For now, I must ask that you not question, just believe."

"Why am I here?"

"I will help you restore your faith in God. Not the god that our religion has taught us to believe in, but God. I will help you fight the evil that lives within your soul and tears away at you in your sleep. I will renew your faith."

Doña Luz held on to the backrest of Anna's chair. Composing herself, she slowly walked towards the bedroom. Anna could hear the doubts floating within her thoughts. She found it surprisingly odd that Doña Luz had not reacted like the Sisters from her days at the Parish School. Doña Luz was different. My only hope, Anna thought.

Doña Luz returned carrying a brown ceramic vase in the shape of a tea kettle. In the vase were two roses. Anna watched as Doña Luz carried the vase with great care. The two roses illuminated as a shiny glowing mist enveloped them. One was a white rose with a soft, snowwhite silky coat. The other, a silky black, like the color of Anna's hair. In the vase lay an ivory rosary that Doña Luz retrieved. She sat down, took Anna's hand, bowed her head in prayer. "Ay Dios y Espíritu Santo..." Anna too, bowed her head in prayer.

Doña Luz lifted her head and began to speak. "Once again my child, I must ask that you not question. I will tell you what you must know for now. I must also ask that you begin to feel the force that you are under without any resistance. Do you understand?"

"Yes"

"I spent the better part of my life serving God as a Sister in the convent. I served the God Catholicism had me serve. My ways are the Catholic way and now it is time that I abolish those beliefs and take back the beliefs of my true nature. My Mamá was a curandera when I was young and before I went to Venice. She taught me her ways and was relieved that I, too possessed the power of the curandera. Upon going to the convent I was forced to store my powers away. It has been over sixty years now, mi hija, since I have used the gifts that God had given me. I will use them now. It is from Mamá that I inherited the vase and the two roses which are placed within it. With these, I also have power, and mi hija, it is going to take all the power in both the vase and in me to bring you back to God. I must warn you that there is a great danger involved. We can only be uncertain of the consequences. I myself am willing to undergo the consequences but it is entirely up to you." Doña Luz looked at Anna in all sincerity. Anna sat quietly, considering Doña Luz's warning.

"I cannot live with this guilt, she replied, "I am willing to try anything."
Anna stared at the roses. How do the roses remain alive after many years,
she wondered.

"The power is within the roses," Doña Luz replied, "They still live.
Mamá saw to that. It is with these roses that we will gain the cure to fight the
evil that surrounds you. These roses, mi hija, will serve to help the guilt go
away. I will give them to you."

Anna paused. "Okay," she said.

"Not so fast my child. You must remember what I have told you. You
must put the ways of the church behind you also. We must call to nature and
its spirit to help. The white rose contains my power. I will be with you
always. You must believe that. The black rose is the most important of the
two. It represents your soul Anna. When you have learned to forgive yourself the rose will transform into the color of purity. When you have gained
forgiveness from God the rose will turn red. Only then, will you be able to
find forgiveness from God."

Anna reached for the vase as Doña Luz's hand pushed it towards her.
"Take this too," she said, handing Anna the ivory rosary. "I think you need
one," she said, winking her eye at Anna.

"Muchas gracias, Doña Luz."

"De nada mi hija."

Anna took the vase. She could feel a force strengthen within her. Doña
Luz will help, she thought, I can already feel a relief. I can already see a hope.

Doña Luz pulled herself out of the chair and reached for Anna's hand.
"Go in peace mi hija."

Anna stood up and walked towards the door. Doña Luz followed. "Muchas gracias, Doña Luz," Anna said, taking her hand, "muchísimas gracias."

"Que Dios te bendiga," Doña Luz said, closing the door behind her.

The Spring days quickly passed by. The nightmares did not return to trouble Anna's sleep. The fear engraved in her eyes seemed to vanish; yet her
soul had not yet found its peace. I must return to Doña Luz's, she thought.

Anna walked through the barrio and towards Doña Luz's home. A group
of boys watched her as she walked on the sidewalk. "Ay, las cosas que hace
Dios," a tall, lanky boy with a blue bandana wrapped around his head yelled,
"qué linda."

The morning glories blossomed to create an arrangement of colors and to conceal the boarded windows of Doña Luz's project home. Anna walked up the steps, almost tripping as the boards of the porch threatened to collapse into the shallow ground. She knocked on the door.

Santiago was playing in the yard next door when he glanced up towards la difunta Doña Luz's porch. He saw Anna standing near the doorway and ran over towards her, "No está," he said.

Anna recognized the little boy, a red kool-aid mustache above his upper lip. "Dónde está Doña Luz?" she asked.

"Se murió la señora anoche," he replied, turning and running back towards his yard.

Anna stepped off the porch and walked. The boys who had yelled to her earlier seemed unnoticeable, as they tried to gain her attention. The morning glories beckoned farewell as Anna turned to glance back at Doña Luz's home. "Go in peace," Doña Luz had said. I only pray that she too, has gone in peace, Anna thought.

Anna arrived to her room and sat on her bed. She glanced towards her desk and watched as the white rose slowly withered, losing the soft silky petals which had once promised hope. The black rose, reminding her; it too, mourning the death of its companion.

She felt a spirit move through her and felt the force leave her to get through this alone. Doña Luz is gone, she thought. The power in the white rose was also gone, as the shriveled petals disintegrated like melting snow. Anna's fear returned, to sustain the power that gave the black rose life. "...The rose will transform into the color of purity when you can find forgiveness within yourself..." Anna looked around, following the spirit that spoke. She tracked the flowing nothingness as it drifted into the beautiful brown ceramic vase to take the place of the withering white rose.

* * * * * * * * * * *

"What is your sin?" Father Ignacio asked.

"I had an abortion, Father."

"That can't be pardoned!"

"But..."

"It doesn't matter!"

* * * * * * * * * * *

Anna stood and watched the spirit flowing into the spout of the vase. The withered white rose vanishing before her eyes. She walked towards the desk and reached for the vase. "Doña Luz?"

Anna took the silky black rose and held it in her hand as she looked into the vase. The smell of roses permeated through the air. She lay the black rose on her New Testament Bible and quickly stepped away as the flames erupted. The smoke flowed amidst the air. Anna pushed the rose off the bible and closed her eyes. Upon opening them she stared at the black leather wrapped bible, its glow making her eyes wince.

Anna placed her hand inside the vase. She touched the bottom and felt the little round ball with her fingers. She grabbed it and pulled it out of the vase and laid it in the palm of her hand. Taking the pea-shaped seed in her hand she observed it. "Doña Luz?"

She placed the seed at the bottom of the vase and walked towards her dresser. She opened the top drawer and took the aspirin bottle which she had filled with holy water on her last visit to the Santuario.

It was as if she already knew what was expected of her as she opened the aspirin bottle, walked towards her desk, and sprinkled the holy water on the seed. She looked into the vase as the seed shed its skin and tiny sprouts erupted from its center. The stem and leaves developed instantaneously and the rose bud appeared. Anna watched the rose bud. The soft white petals would not blossom. She took the black rose from her desk and returned it to the vase. The soft white petals opened, the rose blossomed, and the spirit filled the room, absorbing Anna's spirit within its own.

Anna lifted her head and looked into the mirror above her desk. The image in the mirror suddenly transformed. Doña Luz's blue eyes focused into Anna's. Her smile of hope reassured Anna that she had not left her. The piercing blue eyes no longer told of innocence. The smile lacked its youthfulness.

"Doña Luz?"

"Cómo estás Anna?" she asked, extending her arms out of the mirror in a gesture to embrace her.

The warmth of the embrace replenished Anna's body, returning to it the force that had brought her to Doña Luz. "Anna, you must come with me," Doña Luz said, "there is someplace we must go. Take my hand and come with me.

Anna grasped Doña Luz's hand and felt herself being pulled into the mirror, her image fading as she looked back into the darkness behind her. She could see nothing ahead of her, only darkness as she held on to Doña Luz's hand.

"Doña Luz?"

"Yes, mi hija."

"Where are we going?"

"We are going to my old pueblo of El Purgatorio."

"Why?" Anna asked, increasing her pace to catch up with Doña Luz.

"We must go there to find purification. We can find it no other place but there."

The speck of light amidst the darkness assured Anna that the journey was almost over. "What are we going to do?"

"We are going to God. We must go to God to appeal for your purification. But first we must go to the gods of nature. Did you bring the rosary?"

"No."

Doña Luz stopped and turned to Anna. "We need the rosary. It is too far to go back now. I am losing my strength and have only been granted enough to return to El Purgatorio and return you to your home. We will have to ask the gods of nature to sacrifice another."

"Sacrifice another?"

"Yes. The beads are made of the seeds of nature. Every plant, every herb, and every flower has given of its seed a portion of its life to create the rosary. We must ask the gods of nature to give us another. They are magical seeds Anna, like the one in the vase that brought me to you."

The light blinded Anna's eyes. She turned back to pierce the vast stretch of darkness they had come from. El Purgatorio stood before her as she turned around to follow Doña Luz. The small village resembled her home in El Valle. The old adobe haciendas, the burning firewood stoves, and the old Catholic church appeared extremely small in the midst of the immense mountains which surrounded them.

"We are here," Doña Luz spoke, "we must go to my home. It is there where we can begin."

Anna observed the little village of El Purgatorio. A lost, abandoned village in the northern part of Nuevo Méjico. She could see the Sangre de

Cristo mountains, their snowcapped peaks in the distance. The aroma of burning firewood brought life to the village. The birds chirped a soft melodic tune. The voice could be heard in the distance, but not a human being was in sight.

"Ven," Doña Luz said, taking Anna's hand and leading her towards the North, towards the Sangre de Cristo mountains.

Doña Luz paused to look at the small adobe house in the distance. I am home, she thought, I am home Mamá.

They entered the small adobe hacienda. Doña Luz let go of Anna's hand and speedily walked towards a back door. Standing in the doorway she looked around. "Nothing has changed." she said, as she focused on the fence for penning sheep, the sheds where her papá had kept his farming tools. The old outhouse brought memories of her childhood fear of falling in. "All is as I left," she said, "nothing has changed."

Doña Luz returned to the kitchen where she left Anna to wait. She took a deep breath to absorb the aroma of boiling apples on the firewood stove. Mamá must be making jellies, she thought.

Doña Luz took Anna's hand and led her towards the backyard. Letting go of her hand, she walked towards the old, broken rocking chair which leaned against the wall, rocking back and forth.

"Mamá," Doña Luz said, kneeling at the foot of the rocking chair. "Aquí estoy."

"Bien venida mi hija. Le doy gracias a Dios porque aquí está mi hija. Luz, aquí está tu casa. Aquí está tu alma. ¿ Y quién es ella?"

"Es mi amiga, Mamá. Se llama Anna."

Anna heard Doña Luz and walked towards her, kneeling beside her near the rocking chair. "Who are you talking to?" she asked, "there's no one here."

Doña Luz stared into Anna's eyes. Taking her hand she leaned on her to rise. "We must do this now. We haven't much time. I must soon return to where I came from. Come," she said.

Anna followed her further away from the beaten down adobe hacienda in the distance. Anna looked back. The aroma of fresh jellies and burning firewood was gone. The old rocking chair leaned against the wall in broken pieces. The voices grew louder and not a bird singing could be heard. The signs of life had quickly disappeared.

They walked towards a stream that flowed miles away from the village of El Purgatorio. Doña Luz halted, motioning towards the sky, her arms outstretched, her facial expression pleading for guidance. She reached down and took Anna's hand, as they followed the flow of the stream leading them both to the heart of the Sangre de Cristo Mountains. The walk through the deserted village, over and above hills, fields and waterfalls drew them to the center of the Sangre de Cristo mountains. "We are here Anna," she said, "it is here where I will meet with the gods of nature."

"May we sit for awhile?"

"You are not tired, ven."

Anna followed trying to keep up with Doña Luz's hurried pace. "Are you still tired, mi hija?" Doña Luz asked as she ran her fingers through Anna's hair.

"No," Anna replied, fascinated by the forces and new strength flowing within her. She observed the immense beauty, the stream, the snow white peaks. She bent to reach down, placing her hand in the refreshing stream. She looked towards the distance and saw a vast stretch of roses, black roses, like the one Doña Luz had given to her. "What is that?" she asked, pointing towards the bed of roses that trailed off in the distance.

"We must go there," Doña Luz said, "the gods of nature await us. Those roses represent souls, much like your own, in need of purification. They are waiting for the gods to sacrifice their seeds so that they too can meet God and be granted his forgiveness. You will stand amongst them. I will go speak to the gods, but you must wait here for me.

Doña Luz left, vanishing into the air before Anna could speak. The warmth of the fresh air breathed its own freshness, enveloping Anna into a deep sleep...

...The chants and screams echoed as they welcomed her to hell. It doesn't matter! The umbilical cord which she grasped for life disintegrated in the flames, splitting in half, denying her, as she had denied it. It doesn't matter! Her spirit sank into the flames, screaming in unison with the chants and the cries.

"No!", Anna screamed, her echo like thunder.

Doña Luz bent down towards her. "Wake up Anna," she said, "wake up." Anna became calm in the warmth of Doña Luz's embrace. She remained speechless, eyes focused at the Sangre de Cristo Mountains. She pierced the black bed of roses and felt a relief come over her, mystifying her. The ivory rosary which hung around Doña Luz's neck broke the trance.

"Come my child. You know what you must do. God has made a request."

Anna followed, like a lost shepherd walking in darkness. Upon returning to Doña Luz's home in El Purgatorio, she watched as Doña Luz took the rosary from around her neck and slowly pulled the beads apart. One by one, she dropped them into the flowing stream. Anna watched the smoke erupt from the burning waters. An image like that of the hot springs in Montezuma. "We are finished," Doña Luz said, "we must return now."

The path of darkness guided Doña Luz and Anna. Feeling the heavy push, Anna saw Doña Luz's image as she focused to find her own. "Adiós, Anna," Doña Luz said, as the mirror cracked into tiny pieces.

"What about me?" she asked, her image returning to the shattered mirror.

"You know what you must do," she heard, as she watched the spirit flow out of the ceramic vase.

She looked at the vase. The white rose disappeared before her eyes. Slowly and majestically the black rose transformed into shades of gray, into a clear crystal, and finally into snowy white.

Anna walked towards the dresser and removed the razor blade from her shaver. She took it between her fingers, its coldness drawing her to tightly grasp it. As she looked out the window and turned towards the Sangre de Cristo mountains in the distance, she heard the echo. "It doesn't matter!" Anna took the razor blade and planted it into her wrist, running it across vertically, oblivious of all pain. The echo became louder..."It doesn't matter!"

The blood dripped from her wrist, assembling into a trail and flowing on the floor. It glided towards the bed, above the chair, into the vase, and into the stem of the silky black rose. The black rose slowly transformed into the bloody color of sacrifice, the bloody color of love.

In the distance, amidst the miles and miles of black roses, in the heart of the Sangre de Cristo mountains, in the midst of a peaceful eternity, one could hear the echo...Rosa Blanca, Rosa Negra, Rosa Colorear. In the very heart of the Sangre de Cristo mountains, one could see a snowy white rose and a bloody red one in the center of the vast mileage of surrounding black roses.

"Adiós Anna..." Doña Luz said,"...to God."

* * * * * * * * * * *

For I know the plans I have for you, declares the Lord,
plans to prosper you and not to harm you,
plans to give you hope and a future.

Jeremiah 29:11

Gloria G. Gonzales

Alive and Growing

It was
a
Great
Pity Party
once i
realized
i needed
nurturing
i took it
upon
myself
and myself
did i
nurture.

There Is Nothing

There is nothing
so lonesome
or sad
that
papas fritas
won't cure.

María Dolores Gonzales

She Called It Wiggling

Long black dress
and a hooded hat
eyes holier than thou
with rosary beads in hands.
You are children of God
and must follow his rules,
to get to heaven
you must be good.
WIGGLING is the devil's work
and you'll burn in hell.
Cast him out, cast him out!
If only bad girls wiggle
I was doomed at five.
I wonder how she knew
so much about wiggling?

DOLORES

María. Te busco
entre las voces de
Cota-Cárdenas
entre los colores de
Cisneros
entre las imágenes de
Vigil y de Hoyos.

Te encuentro aquí
entre las hojas
en blanco llorando
de tantos, dolores.

Egos For Sale

This ego used to be firm
and ripe
bright crimson red
that stood out from all
the others on the vine
of life.

Today it is shriveled up
turning brown and even
smells bad.
What a pity it got plucked
before its time.

Erlinda Gonzales-Berry

(Más) Conversaciones Con Sergio

fragmento de novela

Qué rico, Sergio, estar contigo otra vez. Pues te diré la verdad, la playa estuvo divina, pero la especie humana que allí se encuentra, olvídate. En primer lugar, cuando llegamos, claro totalmente aterrorizadas puesto que fue nuestro primer viaje largo por camión, no encontramos taxi que nos llevara al hotel. Por fin, se nos acercó un chavo, de unos veinte años, diría yo, y nos dijo que él nos llevaba. Le preguntamos si era taxista como no llevaba la lucecita esa en el coche y dijo que sí, que su compañía estaba de huelga, pero que él seguía dando jalones clandestinamente—eso, clandestinamente—porque tenía que hacerse la vida. Tú dime, ¿qué íbamos a hacer? Allí estábamos superlistas para pachanguear y abandonadas en la estación de camiones. Pues regateamos un rato y por fin aceptamos. Al subirnos al coche vi que iba manejando otro chico, así todo golfo con su chaquetita de cuero, y el pelo teñido, pues no exactemente rubio sino más bien anaranjado y bien tostadita la piel. Ándale. tipo beachboy. Nos subimos las cuatro, Toña, Lupe, Julie, y yo en el asiento de atrás y el otro chavo adelante. Pues yo ya iba con mis temorcitos de siempre, ¿sabes? pero no dije nada. Y el golfito que no le quitaba los ojos—por el espejo—a Julie. Pues para empezar, no arrancó el coche; allí nomás nos quedamos estacionados un rato. Y yo que qué pasa. Es que allí enfrente está estacionado un super de la compañía y no queremos que nos vea, y el golfito mirando intensamente a Julie por el espejo. Por fin hizo arrancar el coche pero no caminamos a ningún lugar. De pronto vi que el golfito les hacía así a los focos, off-on-off-on, tú sabes, como si estuviera señalando a alguien. Pues más vívida que película en tecni se me presenta en la mente, así comi un flash rápido, una escena a la Macon County Line. ¿A poco esas películas no les llegaron? Menos mal,

no les hace falta ese tipo de porquería. Lo que vi fue una playa desierta, como
que ni siquiera una gaviota, tres coches atacados de golfos circundando el
"taxi" y el golfito pelirojo, aún pelándole el ojo a Julie, saca un enorme
machete a la vez que escupe entre los dientes. Allí las tienen cuates, a todos
menos a la güerita; esa me toca a mí. Y eso fue todo, pero bastó para que me
subiera la presión. Empecé a sudar a la gota gorda. Cuando ya no aguanté:
perdón me siento mareada, tengo que salir. Tan cortés como si fuera ver-
dadero caballero, me abrió la puerta y me dejó salir el otro chavo. Fui direc-
tamente hacia un policía que andaba por allí. Me miró así incrédulo cuando
le dije, pues mire, es que esos chicos ofrecieron llevarnos al hotel pero no sé
si son or si no son taxistas porque se están comportando muy raro. Creo que
están contemplando raptarnos y después ultrajarnos. Usted ¿que sugiere
que hagamos? Toña, mientras tanto, cuando me vio ir hacia el policía, pues,
también se asustó y sacó su navajita—dizque es para pelar frutas y nunca
sale sin ella—por si acaso. Por fin salió el chota de su trance de y-a-esta-
loca-qué-le-picó y le señaló a un taxista que acababa de estacionarse en
frente de la estación. Andale, Chemo, lleva a estas pochas a su hotel, y
ustedes señoritas ya no se anden subiendo con extranjeros (como si Chemito
fuera amigazo de toda la vida). Pues allí vamos hechas peor que sardinas,
esta vez en Volkswagen y el taxista más amable que vendedor de coches
usados. Cuando por fin llegamos al Faro me preguntó Lupe que qué pasó en
la estación. Cuando les conté lo de mi premonición, pues se atacaron de risa
y empezaron a vituperarme con sus ¡ay Mari, tú siempre tan histriónica! Ya
no eres niña. ¿Cómo nos vamos a divertir si tú vas a andar friquiada (tú
sabes, dialecto chicano) y con tus temores y tus pendejadas? Qué ingratas,
¿verdad? Yo acabo de salvarles la vida y esas son las gracias que me dan.
Gracias las del payaso, como diría mami. Pero en fin les dije, bueno, de
ahora en adelante no digo nada; simplemente las sigo a ustedes y a ver hasta
donde llegamos. Right on, Mari y no sé cuanto pedo. Pues ya verás, vida, los
líos en que me metieron esas amiguitas izque liberadas.

 Mira, acomódate. Dame esa almohada. Pon las piernas aquí. ¿Quieres un
frajo? Pásame tu incendador. No, ese no, tontito. Okay, baby. STORYTIME.

 Después de descansar un rato, salimos a la playa. Allí estabamos absor-
biendo vitamina D cuando se acercaron unos alemanes. Empezamos a ma-
derearnos con ellos, que de dónde eran, que qué hacían en Mexicles y todo eso

¿no? Claro que no les dijimos que éramos de allá; les dijimos que eramos de D.F. Cuando ya se había puesto el sol nos convidaron a ir a tomar una copa y después a cenar, pero que primero tenían que pasar por su hotel por dinero. Cuando llegamos al hotel, inmediatamente me dejé caer en una poltrona en el lobby. Hacía un calorazo del infierno afuera. De una vez empezó él que se llamaba Hans con que subiéramos, darlinks, con ellos. Que tenían buen tequila, Noche Buena y Harveys Bristol Cream. Al oír la marca mágica, salté de la silla y todos nos encaminamos hacia el ascensor. Pues nos sirvieron y estuvimos charlando un rato. No, si se les entendía bien. Con muchas eses ápicoalveolares, con la [Θ] castellana y con la elle lateral palatal. Así mira: [Θapato], [eṣpaña], [kaɫe]. En fin muy madrileño su español. Nosotras muy impresionadas porque tenían un suite con dos recámaras, dos baños, sala y cocinita, todo muy arregladito, pues ya sabes cómo son los alemanes. Ya yo iba en mi segunda copa de Harveys cuando pasó Hans a la recámara y salió con una maleta. La abrió, sacó una cámara y un pequeño televisor. Cuando acabó de armar todo el juego me di cuenta que era una cámara de video y allí mismo empezamos a salir en la pantallita de la tele. Lupe de una vez se entusiasmó—ya sabes cómo le gusta estar ante la cámara siendo bailarina y todo. Bueno Toña es un poco tímida y hacía los posible por esconderse, y Julie cool as a cucumber como nomás ella. Tan fresca como un pepino. No, Sergio, no creo que sea alusión sexual, es simplemente una expresión sin sentido. Empezaron todos a jugar con la cámara, claro menos yo. No sé por qué, pero empecé a sentirme un poco incómoda y le dije a Julie: I smell a rat. Me oyó Lupe y no tardó en proclamar ¡ay Mari, deja de hacer escándalos! En eso dice uno de los chicos, creo que se llamaba Peter, ¿No creen que hace demasiado calor aquí? y se quitó la playera quedando en traje de baño y, créeme, amor, esos alemanes llevan lo que se llama bikini. Fíjate que no tienen vergüenza. Pues así dicen, que siempre son ellos los primeros en encuerarse en la Costa del Sol. Pues Lupe, que por allí deber tener sangre alemana, siguió el ejemplo y también se quitó la playera y la falda que se había puesto sobre el traje de baño.Entonces saltó Hans a la cámara y empezó a enfocar sobre Lupe and a gritar *kommt mal, zieht euch auss kleine Häschen* que según Peter quiere decir anden conejitas, quítense la ropa. A mí todo esto me cayó gordo. Llámale intuición o sencillamente sentido común, pero justamente cuando dije yo me voy al hotel, salió Erik de la otra recámara con una P38 Walthur. Es que Steve tenía una. ¿No te he contado lo de Steve? Yo creía que sí. Bueno una de estas tardes te cuento. Entonces dijo Erik, miren muchachos lo que me compré en el mercado esta tarde. En el mercado, ¿tú crees? ¿Les gusta? y me miró a mí al decirlo. I got the message, babe. Volví a sentarme y me quité la playera simulando haber entrado en el juegito que estaba a punto de volverse un poco grotesco. Mis compañeras, pues olvídate, como si anduvieran hipnotizadas. ¡No se daban cuenta de nada! Allí andaban bailando como si jámas hubieran conocido la inhibición, y el maldito ojo de la cámera siguiéndolas. Yo viéndolas en la pantalla, anticipando, horrorizada por dentro, la escena escandalosa que estaba por desarrollarse, y Erik jugando con su Walthur, acariciándola y a cada rato mirando hacia mí. De pronto di con un plan. Salté de la silla y me quité la falda. Claro que traía mi traje de baño, el bikini que tanto te gusta. Corrí y abracé a Hans y empecé a darle besitos en la oreja. Nada retrasado el mensito. Vamos a la recámara. Vamos le dije. ¿Llevamos la cámara? En un rato le dije. A mí gusta un warm-up period. Se rió y me guió hacia la puerta. Nadie se dio cuenta que habíamos salido. Al entrar en la recámara la recorrí rápidamente con los ojos. Cuando me agaché para desenlazarme las sandalias, me arrebató del brazo derecho el bruto, me lo torció detrás de la espalda y me tiró sobre la cama. Hans, Hans, si quieres ser tigre, primero tienes que ser gatito. Con calma le dije. Mira, tú nomás acuéstate aquí y déjame abrirte la puerta a placeras jamás imaginados en climas nórdicos. Nosotras las mexicanas conocemos los secretos eróticos de los aztecas. Secretos pasados a seres escogidos por Coyoxauhqui. Secretos practicados únicamente por vírgenes entrenadas sobre los guerreros prisioneros en víspera de su sacrificio. Abrió unos ojos Hans y dijo ¡O darlink, soy tu prisionero! Del ropero saqué dos camisas, las desgarré, lo amarré a la cama y lo amordacé, pero no antes de haber quitado las sábanas. De la sala oí a alguien gritar en voz amenazante, te dije que te lo quitaras. Eso fue lo que me dio coraje para hacer lo que sabía que tenía que hacer. Rápidamente junté las dos sábanas con un nudo, y la orilla de una la até a la cama. Abrí la ventana; me mareé al mirar hacia la tierra, pero sin más ni más me dejé ir del octavo piso. Nunca me pregunté a dónde pensaba llegar. Afortunadamente la sabana llegaba justamente al balcón del suite inmediatamente debajo del de los alemanes. Cuando oí unos gritidos de señoras bien educadas supe que había gente en el balcón. Dos hombres me tomaron en brazos y me ayudaron a aterrizar en el balcón. Pero muchacha, dijo uno de los señores, hay mejores maneras de suicidarte. Escuchen por favor, necesito ayuda. Rápidamente les expliqué que mis amigas estaban en peligro. Después supe que el señor que fue a la puerta de los alemanas y anunció con máxima autoridad que la señorita Lupe Quiñones tenía una llamada de emergencia en el lobby, era un general del ejército peruano que andaba de vacaciones en Acapulco. Después nos sacaron él y su señora a cenar. ¿Las chavas? Pues salieron así muy ordenaditas como si nada, poniéndose las playeras y despidiéndose de los alemanes, hasta luego muchachos, chaucito, gracias por todo. Los alemanes se quedaron en la puerta con la boca abierta y de los ojos les salía fuego. Al despedir al general en el séptimo piso, empezamos a reír a carcajadas y así salimos del hotel y seguimos a lo largo de la calle hasta llegar al Faro. Y a cada rato decían las muchachas, ¡ay Mari, loquita y escandolosa Mari, nos salvaste de las pezuñas del demonio! Pues me imagino que lo hallarían atado a la cama ¿no?

Bueno después tuvimos algunas experiencias más placenteras. Como te dije, salimos a cenar con el general, y olvidando nuestro plan original de buscar chavos, decidimos gozar de nuestra compañía femenina. En fin, nuestro primer viaje a Sin City Mexico tuvo sus buenos momentos. Pero sabes algo, Sergio, te extrañé un montón. Incluso hablamos mucho de ti. Les extraña tanto a mis amigas que yo pueda ir a donde quiera, que salgo con otras personas si me da la gana, que te cuento todo y que seguimos queriéndonos loca y apasionadamente. Les cuesta mucho creer que no te pones celoso, que no te portas como si yo fuera tu propiedad privada. Siempre terminan diciendo, Sergio no es el chavo típico. En fin, es un tipo que verdaderamente cree en la libertad y que vive su ideología. Es verdad, Sergio; eres muy especial. Y ahora, darlink, soy yo prisionera tuya, así que realiza sobre mi persona tus deseos más ocultos.

Demetria Martínez

Bare Necessities

Coffee, scotch, 2 a.m.,
I live for revelations,

ideas foaming,
cresting into insight.

The litter of life:
books, fights, trips.

Juxtaposed in conversation
so that we see the whole,

this seeing is power.

I do not live
to speak your truths for you.

Laboriously, joyfully
we come

to truth together
or not at all.

Hail Mary

Full of grace, priests crowned you,
1598, with ruddy embers
at the village stake.
1952, your daddy knuckled you
out-of-state where unwed
mamas wheeled strollers to school.
In 1982 you were raped
red, white and blue
by the good troops of El Salvador
who shined their rifles
at cathedral doors.

Witch. You grew herbs
to ease morningsickness,
conversed with angels.
Bitch. You made love with
life instead of a man,
birthed a troublemaker,
you asked for it.

Blessed are you among
women skimming headlines,
reading stars, awaiting
one small portent
of good news.

Discourse on Method

July 10th, my month's blood is bright.
Candle at the tub, knees and breasts
in a bubble reef, reading Blake
by threadbare light.
A child, I dreamed I was a killer whale,
black crescent bellying through seas,
eating shark, bearing young, far
from these altitudes, these
neon years one must bear
until the work is done.

Nightly, my eyes return to their waters,
plunging leagues when I close my lids,
back at dawn with accounts of wrecks,
with fins, coins, remains of men.

Those who learn to see in the dark
never go blind.
It is a good year to be woman
and whale at the same time.

One Dimensional Man

His smile, a minus sign, cancels
whole populations.
I was useful once, a tape recorder
he talked at and played back,
a rear view mirror announcing
his face at stop lights.
On a self-improvement spree
he took me up like tennis
or a Third World cause.
I the colored help,
Guadalupe, quota, folk art,
more chic than a Santa Fe healer
he saw on the sly,
my Guatemalen cottons
matched his ties.

Bastard. Strip-mining wasted
your heart. How you love
to subtract. Ordering soldiers
to save a village you strike
the match. You always liked me
on my back, with an instamatic
you snap, snap. Sentimental,
you pocket my eyeteeth,
you finger my onyx. Liberal,
you do not steal it, you donate
my bracelet to a Mayan exhibit.

Gina Montoya

Math Anxiety

Oh, Math Anxiety — fear of the unknown
Oh, Computer Anxiety — fear of the known Anxiety
of Math, of Computers, of learning,
to weave all those yearnings
into a special little skill, churning
and cranking out the services on a keyboard
praying for the burning
away
of all those bad memories

---change---change---change---

the learning process to interlace with the learning
of working past and working through,
of relieving that old, old feeling of

Oh, Math Anxiety — fear of the unknown
Oh, Computer Anxiety — fear of the known Anxiety

Roberta M. Rael

Wounded Women

We are wounded women marching on a special mission.

We are wounded women marching along a rough and rocky trail.

We are wounded women and we each have our own dogs yapping and biting
at our feet.

We are wounded women and one cries, "Carry me, Carry me."

We are wounded women and one has been bitten so badly she is crippled—
yet, she marches on.

We are wounded women and one yells, "I am falling, I am falling," as she
lies on the ground.

We are wounded women and one's spirit is elsewhere.

We are wounded women and one carries her load quietly, hoping it will
lighten.

We are wounded women and one cries out as her tired feet blister and the
puss oozes out.

We are wounded women and one studies the situation and walks carefully
so as not to be sucked into the vacuum of anger, self-pity, and pain.

We are wounded women and *my* wounds hurt.

We are wounded women and I wonder *why* we are marching.

We are wounded women and I wonder if I will ever sparkle again.

Laura Gutiérrez Spencer

Mujer

Mujer
tu nombre
es:

Beata   Bruja
Santucha   Puta
Rígida   Suelta
Pesada   Liviana
Vanidosa   Greñuda
Gorda   Tísica
Creída   Cohibida
Fría   Caliente

Dos caminos se abren a tus pies
La ruta del dominio, la vía de la infamia
Y entre los dos un ancho trecho
El abismo de la madre-virgen
Encarnación fantasmal
Del verbo inventado
Por el hombre-dios
La perfecta incongruencia
Que nos subyugó
A la doble herida
De la serpiente
De la lengua bifurcada

Schariar

Sentados juntos en la sombra yo te
Contaba un cuento de *Las mil y una noches*
Hasta me di cuenta que la historia repetida
Estaba encantando a ti
Hechizador, sultán de erotismo.
Espero en tu jaula, embrujada por tu voz de pardo terciopelo
Rayando rejas en mi cuento, presintiendo el calor de tus caricias.
Empezó a aclarar la niebla de tu melancólica soledad
Zandunga me llamaste y en tu sueño estiraste la mano hacia mí
Alejándome un poco, detrás del velo de encaje aun no te
Dejé que conocieras el fin de la historia, ni
El nombre de mi clave

Cada Noche

Sueño de él que me leía cuentos de hadas
Me llevaba a parques infantiles
Y me enseñaba los interiores de palacios fabulosos

Cada noche yo tengo que luchar
Con pesada espada
Contra monstruosos dragones
Que se asoman a mi ventana

Y después de amanecer
Sudando y rendida
Me alegro a ver la luz del día

Mi hermanita esperó en la sombra hasta que yo la busqué
Y desde entonces me toma de la mano
Cada noche y me lleva hacia abajo
A mirar el negro espejo

Donde él me pinta en cuadros desnuda,
Desfigurada, y de cara muda
Cada noche me da el retrato de obsequio fatal
Que escondí tras el muro del olvido

Cada noche yo tengo que luchar
Con pesada espada
Contra monstruosos dragones
Que se asoman a mi ventana

Recuerdo a él que me leía cuentos de hadas
Me llevaba a parques infantiles
Y me enseñaba los interiores de palacios fabulosos

Porque érase una vez
Que él abrió la puerta al abismo
Y me obligó a mirar

Francisca Tenorio

Inflight

The veil lifted and she was reborn.
A breath filled her lungs...
    her spirit sang.
Caught in his web
  for such a long, long time...
entangled,
    though not alone....
for he was always with her
and together they fed upon each other
    as black widows do.
Survival was unthought...unplanned...
  then she awoke
    in the fog-filled forest
     they called love,
      that they called L-O-V-E...
     yes, love.
She emerged from the cacoon they'd spun
and lived in for so long.
She spread her wings and flew away.
   For him it was more difficult.
    He never wanted it to end...
     he never wanted her to leave.

Rock-A-Bye

We shared some memories
    long before you were ever born.
I remember how I felt
    when I first knew you were alive
        inside of me.
You were conceived
    in erotic frenzy
        two wet bodies
            melting into one.
In my fantasies
    you were given life
        a searing orgasm.
Your spirit exploded...
    nestled warmly in my womb
as I snuggled in his arms
    breathing like the cloudy flutter
        I felt stirring inside
    you stretched and reached
to grasp this world outside.
You began, grew and arrived
    in pain and pleasure...
        and, so its been
            throughout the years.
We've shared so much of both.

Cecile Turrietta

Haciendo Turismo En Vidas Ajenas

I can hear Maite's voice. She is arguing with her father who is the owner of this modest pension in the Casco Viejo of Bilbao. The old man is set in his ways and tells his daughter he likes his food "hot" not tepid. Maite is 31. She and her husband, a machinist, have agreed to live in the pension for two weeks while Maite's mother takes their ten year old son on vacation to a mountain resort in Asturias.

Besides their ten year old son, this couple have a three year old daughter with cerebral palsy. The child has had several operations in Spain and one in France, yet her condition has worsened. Her right leg hangs limp or tenses up and will not bend. Her left hand is wrapped in a tight fist or flies around like a bird above her head. She still wears diapers and cannot feed herself. The child cannot speak other than to repeat "ama," which in the Basque language, means "mother." Maite feels the girl is very intelligent and believes she will one day be able to read. She may not have the capacity to walk.

Although she is only three, the child is difficult to hold in my arms. Her back, and particularly her neck, must always be supported. The electrical impulses in her little body start up unexpectedly and with such force that she can easily throw me off balance. I must brace myself against a wall to keep from falling with her. She is a lovely girl. Her laughing eyes and winning smile are as hopeful as those of all children with caring relatives. I can only wonder what her fate will be here in Spain. Body braces at seven, a wheel chair by ten, institutionalization at 15. ¿Qué quinceañera es eso?

Maite really wanted this second baby. Her husband felt they could not afford to have a second child. Now Maite feels very guilty. Guilty for insist-

ing on having a baby—guilty for the child's illness,—guilty for the emotional
and financial burden on the family. As soon as it was understood that the
baby had cerebral palsy, Maite arranged to have her tubes tied.

The child requires 24-hour attention. Maite's husband, son, and father
also demand her attention. Nobody helps her with the housekeeping. After
all, it is women's work. By the time she goes to bed she is exhausted, but her
husband is not. She wants to sleep. He wants to talk. Maite was afraid she
might be frigid. It has been almost two years since she enjoyed sexual intercourse, but she agrees to it willingly. Her voice faltered when she said that
she abolutely detests having anal intercourse with her husband because it
hurts physically. So why doesn't she tell him all of this? She is afraid he will
find someone else who complains less and has more energy.

"Maite, de dónde sacas el coraje y valor de seguir arreglando la vida para
que tu familia lo puede pasar bien?'

La pregunta en el silencio se quedó. Juan Manuel, el esposo de Maite
llego del trabajo y quería su cafe.

Claror Lunar II
Pastel and Silver Aluminum Powder—Ana María Mastrogiovanni

Contributors

Marian Baca Ackerman grew up in Las Vegas, New Mexico, attended Loretto Academy in Santa Fe, and graduated from Loretto Heights College in Denver with a degree in English and Drama. She is a language arts teacher at West Las Vegas Middle School.

Mary Montaño Army, a former arts writer and critic for the *Albuquerque Journal*, is an arts administrator for Opera Southwest and 'Viva Zarzuela!, a Spanish comic opera company in Albuquerque, New Mexico.

Elena Avila R.N., M.S.N. was born and raised in El Paso, Texas. She is the parent of four children and lives in Rio Rancho, New Mexico. She incorporates natural healing techniques in her private practice, and presents workshops on curanderismo.

Maya Gonzales Berry is a full time student majoring in Communications and Spanish. She is currently studying at the University of Granada in Spain.

Elba C. De Baca is from Las Vegas, New Mexico. She is a retired school teacher and lives in Mineral Hill.

Cordelia Chávez Candelaria is Associate Professor in the English Department and Interim Director, Center for Studies of Ethnicity and Race at the University of Colorado at Boulder. Among her recent publications are *Chicano Poetry, A Critical Introduction* and *Ojo de la Cueva/ Cave Springs*, a chapbook.

Delfina Faver Rede Chávez was born in 1910 in Shafter, Texas. She studied in Mexico, receiving her M.A. degree at New Mexico State University. She moved to Las Cruces in 1944 to teach Spanish in the public schools. She taught for 42 years throughout Texas and New Mexico.

Denise Chávez, a native of Las Cruces, New Mexico, is the author of *The Last of the Menu Girls*. She is a professor in the Drama Department at the University of Houston.

Margo Chávez is a native of Las Cruces, New Mexico. She is a graduate student in the American Studies Department at the University of New Mexico.

tesamaechávez was born in Albuquerque and in fourth grade moved to Aztec, New Mexico. She attended the University of New Mexico and TVI. At present she lives in Port Isabel, Texas.

Josephine M. Córdova is the author of *No Lloro Pero Me Acuerdo*. She was born in Arroyo Seco, New Mexico, and was a school teacher for forty years.

Kathryn M. Córdova is an English and government and law teacher at Taos High School, Taos, New Mexico. She worked for the News Bureau of the Highlands University, the *Alpha News* in Las Vegas, New Mexico, and the *Santa Fe News*. She was a free-lance writer for the *Taos Magazine*, and the editor of *No Lloro Pero Me Acuerdo* by Josephine M. Córdova.

Elvera Adolfita De Baca lives in Los Lunas, New Mexico. In 1980 she ran for New Mexico State Representative. She writes for the Albuquerque Hispano Chamber of Commerce Newsletter.

Reynalda Ortiz y Pino de Dinkel lives in Santa Fe, New Mexico. She received her BA and MA degrees from the University of New Mexico. She taught Spanish in the Santa Fe School System for over thirty years.

Tina Fuentes has a MFA with a concentration in drawing and painting. She taught for several years at the University of Albuquerque. After teaching one year at UNM she joined the Art Faculty at Texas Tech in Lubbock. She maintains her studio in Albuquerque. Her most recent exhibition has been in the New Mexico Hispanics in the United States.

Lorena García was born in Chile. She received her BA degree in creative writing from the University of New Mexico. She lives in Isleta, New Mexico.

Marcella Lucinda García is from Portales, New Mexico. She received her degrees in psychology and English from the University of New Mexico.

María Dolores Gonzales, born in Springer, New Mexico, attended schools in Rosebud and El Rito. She is a doctoral candidate in the Department of Modern and Classical Languages at the University of New Mexico.

Erlinda Gonzales-Berry was born and raised in Northeastern New Mexico. She attended high school in El Rito and received her Ph.D. from the University of New Mexico where she teaches in the Department of Modern and Classical Languages.

Gloria Gonzales-Garofalo, parent of four children, lived in Ribera, New Mexico, in the Pecos River Valley for fourteen years. She now lives in Santa Fe.

Margaret Herrera (Chávez) studied art at Highlands University, the University of New Mexico, and the Instituto Allende in Mexico. A native of Las Vegas, New Mexico, she has exhibited widely. In 1987 she was honored as a visual artist at the Fiesta Artística.

Juanita Jaramillo Lavadie, a norteña de nuevo méjico and a former muralista, is a weaver of fresadas de lana. She lives in Taos.

Elida A. Lechuga was born in Albuquerque, New Mexico. She has degrees in English from New Mexico State University and the University of New Mexico. She has published in *Voces*.

Soledad Marjon received an MFA in photography from the University of New Mexico in 1982. She has had numerous exhibitions of her hand painted photographs and is currently one of eight New Mexico artists exhibited in "Expresiones Hispanas."

Demetria Martínez, a native New Mexican, is a poet and a free-lance writer for the *Albuquerque Journal*'s religion section, and the *National Catholic Reporter*. Her first book, *Turning*, a collection of poetry will be published by Bilingual Press.

Ana María Mastrogiovanni, a graphic artist, designer and scenic painter has a B.F.A. from the University of Albuquerque. Born in Argentina she has lived in Albuquerque since 1975. She has won awards for portrait and figure drawing and currently is working as a free-lance artist.

Delilah Merriman is a print maker and photographer. She has won many awards for her work and has exhibited extensively. She is doing graduate work in Art at the University of New Mexico. She works as a medical photographer.

Ciria S. Montoya was born in Casa Colorado, New Mexico and grew up in Armijo, New Mexico. Now retired, she worked for thirty years for the Federal Government. Currently she is working on an autobiography.

Linda Montoya was born in Santa Fe, New Mexico where she still lives. She received her education at New Mexico State University, the Art Institute of Boston, and the College of Santa Fe. She has exhibited widely.

Regina Montoya was born in Albuquerque and is a student at the University of New Mexico. She is an advocate for the Rape Crisis Center, has worked with MANA and coordinated Hispanas in Higher Education.

Rosalie Otero was born in Taos, New Mexico. She received her Ph.D. in English from the University of New Mexico. Her work has been published in *Voces* and *The Third Woman: Minority Women Writers of the United States*.

Marihelen Ponce lives in Albuquerque, New Mexico where she is a doctoral candidate in American Studies at the University of New Mexico. She is the author of *Taking Control*. Her short stories have appeared in journals and collected works.

Roberta M. Rael graduated from the University of New Mexico. She has worked at the Shelter for Victims of Domestic Violence in Albuquerque. Questa, New Mexico is her hometown.

B.K. Rodríguez is a native New Mexican. She is a visual artist trained in Mexico City in fine art and mural painting. She is Director of the Fiesta Artística (1988) for the City of Albuquerque.

Vicki Lynn Saiz, born and raised in Santa Fe, New Mexico, is a student at the University of New Mexico. Her writing has been influenced by Rudolfo Anaya and Pat Mora.

Irene Barraza Sánchez, born in Gallup, New Mexico, is the author of *Comida Sabrosa-Homestyle Southwestern Cooking*. She now lives in Tomé.

210

Juanita M. Sánchez, a native New Mexican, is a machinist, a curandera and a poet. She is a resident of Albuquerque.

Linda Sandoval is from Santa Fe, New Mexico. She is a student, in English and journalism, at the University of New Mexico. She also does work in children's literature, taking correspondence classes from the Institute of Children's Literature.

Nell Soto Sehestedt received a Master of Arts degree from California State University, San Bernadino. Her short stories have won a first and second prize from the Writers Association, Joshua Tree, California, and the *Hi Desert Star*, respectively.

Laura Gutiérrez Spencer is from Silver City, New Mexico. She is a doctoral candidate in Spanish at the University of New Mexico.

Francisca Herrera Tenorio, a native of Albuquerque, received her BA and MA degrees in education at the University of New Mexico. Her work has been published in *Voces*, *San Marcos Review*, *Southwest Tales* and *Hispanic Humanities in the Schools*.

Yolanda Troncoso is from Las Vegas, New Mexico. She is a student at the University of New Mexico and works at the UNM Zimmerman Library.

Cecile Turrietta lives in Albuquerque, New Mexico. She received her BA and MA degrees from the University of New Mexico in Latin American Studies and counseling, respectively. She is the producer of a video tape on and about Sabine Ulibarrí's literary works.

Carol Usner is a graduate student in the Department of Modern and Classical Languages at the University of New Mexico. She was born and raised in Northern New Mexico.